RJ

22

B

Alderson 4/18

D1646561

700033809368   3

Tenbury
January 2016

SPECIAL MESSAGE TO READERS

THE ULVERSCROFT FOUNDATION
(registered UK charity number 264873)

was established in 1972 to provide funds for
research, diagnosis and treatment of eye diseases.
Examples of major projects funded by
the Ulverscroft Foundation are:-

* The Children's Eye Unit at Moorfields Eye
  Hospital, London
* The Ulverscroft Children's Eye Unit at Great
  Ormond Street Hospital for Sick Children
* Funding research into eye diseases and
  treatment at the Department of Ophthalmology,
  University of Leicester
* The Ulverscroft Vision Research Group,
  Institute of Child Health
* Twin operating theatres at the Western
  Ophthalmic Hospital, London
* The Chair of Ophthalmology at the Royal
  Australian College of Ophthalmologists

You can help further the work of the Foundation
by making a donation or leaving a legacy.
Every contribution is gratefully received. If you
would like to help support the Foundation or
require further information, please contact:

THE ULVERSCROFT FOUNDATION
The Green, Bradgate Road, Anstey
Leicester LE7 7FU, England
Tel: (0116) 236 4325

website: www.foundation.ulverscroft.com

LEAP YEAR

Tired of the city rush, Erin Mallowson takes a twelve-month lease on Owl Cottage in Norfolk to run her own image consultancy business. Her ex-boss and commitment-phobic boyfriend Spencer thinks she's mad. Keen to embrace the village lifestyle, Erin doesn't expect it to include the enigmatic Brad Cavill, a former footballer with a troubled past. But even though work and love refuse to run smoothly, it turns out to be a leap year that Erin never wants to end . . .

MARILYN FOUNTAIN

LEAP YEAR

Complete and Unabridged

LINFORD
Leicester

First published in Great Britain

First Linford Edition
published 2013

Copyright © 2013 by Marilyn Fountain
All rights reserved

A catalogue record for this book is available
from the British Library.

ISBN 978–1–4448–1792–8

Published by
F. A. Thorpe (Publishing)
Anstey, Leicestershire

Set by Words & Graphics Ltd.
Anstey, Leicestershire
Printed and bound in Great Britain by
T. J. International Ltd., Padstow, Cornwall

This book is printed on acid-free paper

March Arrivals

Erin Mallowson's hand was trembling as she held out the key to Owl Cottage, but the lock turned easily and the door swung open without noise. She released her breath and found herself smiling. This was it. Home! For the next life-changing 12 months, at least.

She could hardly believe she'd actually done it — handed in her notice and sub-let her third-floor Manchester apartment to follow her dream of living and working in the countryside. To find a more meaningful way of life.

While she was still savouring the moment on the threshold, a voice sang out, 'Coming through. Mind your back!'

She stepped inside and flattened herself against the wall, allowing Pete Carr, the local man with the van who'd brought her and her possessions over to Norfolk from Manchester, to carry in the first of the cardboard boxes.

'Where to? Whoops, right here, I suppose.'

She followed his interested gaze round the small front room, leading to the even smaller kitchen area beyond. The slightly uneven walls were painted magnolia and the floor was covered in an oatmeal-coloured carpet. A cast-iron wood-burning stove was tucked into a narrow fireplace. The modern, bland-style furniture comprised a boxy, tan-coloured sofa and a coffee table, sideboard and bookcase in a pale wood. Despite being on a miniature scale, they effectively filled the room.

With Owl Cottage, what you saw was very definitely what you got. Upstairs, she knew from the letting agent's online photographs, was the bedroom and bathroom, their dimensions identical to the rooms beneath.

'The original two-up, two-down. I think it's what they call compact and bijou,' she said with a wry grin.

'You can say that again.' Pete gave a

low whistle from between crooked teeth. 'I've never been inside Owl Cottage before. Old Miss Boyd lived here for years and years. Cor, she was a character! Kept herself to herself, she did. Never used the front door in case any of the cats got out.' He shook his head and grinned. 'Of course, they ran riot in the wheat fields out the back, mousing and whatnot. The place has been smartened up by a developer since then.'

Erin's nose wrinkled. The faint trace of new paint still lingered in the air. But nothing else, thankfully. No smell of damp, which was the main thing she'd always associated with older properties. If there'd been any problems like that with the cottage, the developer had sorted it.

'A great-nephew, or distant cousin or somebody inherited this place, I can't remember which, though Daph will know,' Pete burbled. 'But he was somewhere abroad, anyway. We watched them bring it into the twenty-first century. Still tiny, though, isn't it?'

'Just as well, Pete,' Erin said, just about keeping up, 'otherwise it would have been out of my budget. And I'm like your Miss Boyd, all by myself. Not even a cat to accommodate! So it's plenty big enough for me.'

It really would be fine. She was used to coping in restricted spaces. She'd grown accustomed to living in small flats — ever since she'd started work, in fact. True, success had most recently brought her the luxury of a decent apartment in a fashionable, purpose-built block, but she'd quickly learned that the 'minimalist lifestyle' the development brochure had boasted of was just a way of branding rather superior rabbit hutches!

Small it might be, but Owl Cottage had the character she craved. And Erin was hoping that, once she'd unpacked and spread out her things, perhaps added a few knick-knacks, she would transform the interior space from bland and echoey to cute and cosy.

And there was no time to start like the present. Erin peeled off her jacket to hang on the hook rack behind the door, and noticed some post on the floor. Her very first mail in her new home! Thrilled, she picked up the envelopes. A couple of them felt like greetings cards, and one was addressed with the tell-tale handwritten scrawl of her sister, Elaine. Smiling, she put them all on the sideboard to open and enjoy later.

First things first.

'Cup of tea, Pete?' She headed through to the kitchen sink with the carrier bag containing the essentials. She began opening cupboard doors, hoping to find a kettle somewhere amongst the fixtures and fittings.

'I'll say, Erin,' he said gratefully. 'It seems a long time since that service station snack, don't it?'

They'd fallen into an easy familiarity on the trip. She'd been lucky to find someone from the village to help her make this move. And now, after hearing all about Pete, his wife, Daph, and their grown-up son and daughter, not to mention some of the local gossip, Erin already felt part-way familiar with the community she was joining. She was looking forward to exploring Brundenham for herself as soon as possible.

'Have a break before you bring the rest of my stuff in,' she urged Pete, handing him a steaming mug. 'If you give me a minute to make us up a few sandwiches then I'll give you a hand.'

'That you won't,' he said firmly. 'It won't take me a jiffy to bring in your few bits and bobs.' He waggled his mobile phone in the air. 'But I'll just give Daph a quick ring to tell her we made it home safe and sound.'

Erin couldn't see a landline phone anywhere in the cottage, though there was a socket for one in the wall by the front window. Outside, a cable over-hung the garden leading to a telegraph pole in the street. The letting agent's particulars had promised a good broad-band service in the area, something she'd certainly need to get her business up and running as soon as possible. Tomorrow would be the day for unpacking and setting up her laptop.

Until then, she had her mobile phone. She fetched it from her bag. No calls, no messages. So Spencer hadn't tried to get in touch, or even send his good wishes! He must still be angry at what he considered her abandonment of him, both professionally and personally.

That rankled. Professionally, as an employee of Spencer Riggs's corporate image consultancy business, Erin had every right to hand in her notice and leave. And personally? Well, Spencer had made it quite clear that, as far as he was concerned, their casual personal relationship was fine just as it was, too.

He might have been content continuing with the arrangement, but Erin had found herself wanting something else. Commitment? Perhaps, but more than that. Taking her mug back to the kitchen sink, she put the phone down and gazed out through the back window to the fields, trees and countryside beyond. Never mind about a paradise for cats, all her life Erin had dreamed of living somewhere with a view like this.

It was March, the first of what Erin considered to be the spring months, though there was little sign of that at the moment. The trees were still gangly black silhouettes against a lowering sky, and the fields were neat, rich, brown furrows of apparently bare soil. But it was all happening, just under the surface, and she felt a ripple of exhilaration at the thought of all that new life on the cusp of bursting through out there.

'And in here,' she murmured to herself, pressing her palm against her heart.

Her other hand was still resting on the phone. Should she ring Spencer to tell him she'd arrived safely? She liked to think he would care. But then again, he'd think she was crazy. Manchester to

Norfolk — it was hardly the other side of the world, was it? Even if it did feel a bit like that. The scenery alone, ever since they'd left the motorways and joined the rural roads, gave the impression of being in a different country, never mind county!

According to Spencer she was halfway to crazy already, chucking over the tried and tested familiar for the insecurity of the unknown.

Noticing the time on the phone's display, Erin changed her mind yet again. It was only just after five o'clock. He'd be up to his eyes in work at the office for another couple of hours at least. She had a sudden memory of the hectic office atmosphere, the interrupted deskside snacks that always tasted of traffic fumes, the constant drone from the nearby ring road. Spencer loved the buzz of 24-hour living and working, but Erin had grown to detest everything about it.

When the phone rang, she jumped. Was it Spencer, after all?

It was her sister.

'Elaine! Thanks for your card. I've not had time to open it yet. We've only just come in the door.'

'Oh!' Elaine squealed. 'You got there OK? Is the cottage gorgeous? Do the locals bite?'

'Yes, yes, and not so far.' Erin grinned, glancing over at Pete who was deep into his phone conversation with his beloved wife, Daph. 'Next question.'

'How soon can I come and stay?'

'As soon as you can get here, you know that. Though you'll all have to sleep like sardines in the one bed! Or else standing up . . . ' Erin glanced at the low ceiling and envisaged her brother-in-law's six-foot-four frame.

Elaine gave an exaggerated sigh.

'Oh, Erin, you are lucky. I do envy you your leap year. I think I'll have to park the old man and the boys with mum-in-law and come over and join you.'

'Yeah, right!' Erin snorted, knowing Elaine revelled in the comfort and closeness of her family.

'Do you remember we used to say that, when we grew up, we'd share a London bedsit and live the high life? Whatever happened to those dreams?'

Erin tucked the phone under her ear as she tied back her long, fair hair into a simple ponytail.

'You met the man of your dreams instead.'

'Well, yes, him!' The love in Elaine's voice told Erin that Graham was probably within eyesight. 'While we're on the subject, any word from Spencer?'

'Not so far.'

'Good riddance to him, then,' Elaine snapped succinctly. 'Do you think he'll come around to your point of view in the end?'

Erin suddenly felt weary.

'I really don't know what to think.'

★ ★ ★

By the time Erin came off the phone, Pete had brought in the rest of her belongings.

'There, I told you it wouldn't take long. Daph says you could have come to ours for your tea, but we're off to the football match in Norwich tonight, and we usually pick up something to eat in the ground at half-time.'

Erin was almost silenced by Pete and Daph's thoughtfulness. He'd only just got to know her, and Daph not at all.

'That's so kind, Pete. Thanks to both of you. But I'll be fine for tonight.'

Apart from the tea and coffee things and some fruit, she'd also brought bread with her and a few tins. She planned on having something quick on toast for her first evening. Tomorrow, she'd stock up on food at the small shop Pete had pointed out to her on the drive through the village.

'Now, you've got our phone number, and you know where we are if you need anything,' Pete said when everything she'd brought with her was indoors and he was about to leave.

Erin smiled from the sofa, where she'd temporarily collapsed.

'Second bungalow past the church.' He'd told her three times already.

He nodded.

'Drop by and say hello to Daph when you get a chance. Don't leave it too long, now. And no, don't get up,' he said, opening the door and turning to say goodbye. 'All the best in your new home.' He tapped the doorframe. 'Good little old cottage, this. I think it's going to suit you, girl, living here.'

'I hope so. Thanks, Pete,' she said. 'You've been an absolute brick. And I hope your team wins tonight.'

With a raise of his eyebrows he was gone, but was back again before he'd even closed the door.

'I've just noticed the *To Let* sign's still up outside. I could pull that out, if you wanted, or would you like to do the honours yourself?'

She nodded gleefully.

'As soon as I get up again, it'll be my first job.'

Then he really was gone, and Erin was alone. She leaned back, closed her eyes and allowed her mind free rein. Would she feel scared and lonely, begin to regret making such a move? Certainly there might be times like that ahead, but right now there was just too much practical stuff pressing. There was masses to do, like making the bed, hanging up her clothes, finding a place for everything in the kitchen and the bathroom and familiarising herself with the central-heating and hot-water system. She was desperate for a shower and to get changed out of the practical but shabby tracksuit she'd been wearing all day.

Then there was the stuff that didn't have to be done, but which she wanted to do, just because it was novel and exciting. Like laying the woodburner and lighting a fire, exploring the small back garden . . .

A knocking at the door roused her and for a split second she couldn't think where she was. Then it came to her in a flash. She hadn't realised she'd nodded off but she couldn't have been asleep for very long. The day had been closing in when Pete Carr had left. Now it was dusk, but the room wasn't in complete darkness yet. She must get a torch now she was living in the country. No street lamps here!

Whoever it was knocked again while she was blundering across the room, still feeling slightly disorientated and distinctly crumpled.

'Coming!'

She pressed both light switches simultaneously, which lit up the overhead bulb in the sitting-room and another lamp outside under the porch, and opened the door.

'Hello?'

Her caller was a tall, slim man of around thirty or so, with short, tidy, fair hair. She saw him take a startled half-step back, while whatever it was he'd prepared to say seemed to get stuck in his throat. But he rapidly took another short breath and spoke.

'I've come about renting the cottage. Would it be convenient to have a quick look round now?'

Erin stared at him, the wind completely taken out of her sails.

'No, it's not!' She'd only been there an hour, yet already she was feeling proprietorial about Owl Cottage. 'I'm sorry,' she said with more softness, 'but it's no longer available.'

She raised a hand to her dishevelled hair that was again escaping its black stretchy band.

'Actually, I've only just moved in myself this afternoon.'

He blinked. The bulb in the porch lamp wasn't very strong and she couldn't see the colour of his eyes.

'But you can't have.' He indicated something in the garden. She leaned to look around him and caught sight of the pale banner leaning drunkenly by the gate. The letting agent's sign.

'I meant to take that down,' she said. 'Sorry,' she added eventually, because he seemed rooted to her doorstep.

He rubbed a finger behind his ear and frowned.

'I don't understand this. I was told I had first option on the cottage. It was supposed to be all arranged.'

His words suggested annoyance, anger, even, but she detected a tinge of resignation, too. It was almost as if he'd expected to be disappointed.

'I'm sorry,' she repeated. 'I don't know anything about that.'

Still he stood there.

'Perhaps you should contact the agent?' she suggested. She began inching backwards and making a show of closing the door.

His mouth tightened.

'I will. First thing in the morning.' Now he did sound more decisive, his expression more determined. 'And I expect they'll be in touch with you soon after to sort it out.'

He turned and made his way down the short gravel path to the road, leaving Erin standing there in surprise. She could have called after him. She could have said if he wanted to make a fight of it, she had possession of Owl

17

Cottage, and possession was nine-tenths of the law. Except she wasn't sure that that had any legal basis, and she didn't think of it until much later, anyway. Not until she was standing by the stove and waiting for her bread to brown under the grill and her saucepan of baked beans to warm through.

She couldn't explain why the image of the man's final expression — part-angry, part-disappointed, part-resigned — had stuck in her brain. Or why she kept dwelling on the image of him heading towards the road. There had been a slight hesitation in his walk, a suggestion of a limp, perhaps. But it might only have been the camber of the path. There wasn't the slightest need to feel sorry for him just because he'd lost out on the cottage he seemed to have set his heart on. Nor because he might have a limp.

She shook herself. Tiredness, that was what it was, despite her short nap. Not surprising after such a long, emotional day. She'd be spark out the minute her head hit the pillow . . . except that the bed had still to be made up.

After her scratch supper, she left the saucepan and plate in the sink and headed upstairs with an armful of bed linen. A quaint staircase ran from behind a brace and ledger door by the fireplace and curved behind the chimney up to the first floor. The treads opened out directly into the room, with the bathroom leading off it. That would have once have been a box room or a nursery, she guessed.

An iron-framed bed was tucked under the eaves, leaving the gable end free for a pine wardrobe with a petite dressing-table beside it. The room would benefit from a rearrangement of the furniture, but that was another job for her To Do list.

After hastily making up the bed, she dragged herself into the shower before putting on a pair of cosy pyjamas. Then she remembered she hadn't locked up, so went back down to check both doors.

Upstairs again, she opened the front window that overlooked the lane and savoured the still, velvety night, the sky glittering with stars. A few lights were shining from homes nearer the village centre. Perhaps one of them belonged to Pete and Daph Carr. But in the specific little place on earth that Erin now called home, everything was dark and very peaceful. The crisp, chilly air hit the back of her throat, and Erin snuggled contentedly into her fleecy dressing-gown.

Her hand on the latch, she was about to close the window when she heard it. It wasn't the stereotypically crisp 'tu-whit, tu-whoo', but a rather more frilly, vibrato version. It was also quite faint, somewhere away over the rooftop, coming perhaps from the woodlands out back across the fields. But it was unmistakeably the call of an owl. The owl of Owl Cottage! Erin, delighted, laughed quietly to herself.

It hooted a couple more times, paus-ing between each one, and she wondered if it was waiting for a mate to answer. Erin waited until her hand grew frozen on the latch. It seemed as if the serenade was over for tonight, and reluctantly she closed the window.

Turning, she tumbled into bed, expecting sleep to come instantly. And it almost did . . . after just a few moments mulling over the fact that she'd managed to make both a friend and an adversary on her very first day in the village.

April Surprises

Erin turned the page over on the calendar to April and rehung it on the larder door. The picture was of a rainbow reflected in a puddle. She peered out of the kitchen window at a bright and breezy, if chilly, day. No April showers in Brundenham as yet. Good! She wanted to get on in the front garden this morning. She had a tray of sweet-pea seedlings that needed planting out.

Pete Carr's wife, Daph, had given them to her. Daph's passion in life, apart from football — and Pete, of course — had turned out to be gardening. She was always turning up with spare seedlings, plants, cuttings, and plenty of helpful advice. Erin was determined to do her proud by turning the narrow strip at the front into a typical cottage-style riot of colour, and the back garden into a productive veg patch.

The couple had been good friends to her from day one. Erin blessed her good fortune in finding Pete in the first place, to assist her cross-country move.

It was hard to believe that nigh on a whole month had passed since she'd arrived. She would have liked to think Owl Cottage was unrecognisable since that day, but it wasn't. Not yet. She'd discovered there was a definite knack to the art of achieving the country-cottage look, and it wasn't one she seemed to possess. She'd hung gingham curtains and bought checked cushions for the sofa, arranged bright pictures to do the same for the walls and placed a series of rose-patterned jugs along the deep window-sills. But everything had yet to blend together.

It was still very early days. Except that the time did seem to pass quickly in the country, definitely more speedily than in town. In Manchester, the evenings stretched long into the night, with clubs and bars staying open late. Out here, the evenings still came early, and it was so tempting to settle down with a book or a supper tray on her knee in front of the woodburner.

Daph had put her on to the local timber merchant, who'd delivered a half load of suitable logs and bags of smaller kindling. Erin had spent a weekend's labour stacking it all in the tumbledown wood store outside the kitchen door.

This was after she'd negotiated a working relationship with the resident cockerel. 'Napoleon', as she'd christened him, due to his short stature and strutting gait, had adopted the garden as his own. Enquiries in the lane and a postcard on the village notice board, had brought forward no owner.

'Looks like we're stuck with each other,' Erin told him, after Daph explained that people always had too many cockerels and that, if he hadn't either escaped or been given his freedom, he could very well have ended up in the pot.

By then, Erin had grown rather fond of Napoleon.

'Just don't wake me up too early, OK?' she'd warned.

Napoleon had blinked back inscrutably. Fortunately, he'd turned out to be rather a late riser. Often he was still dozing on the wood pile when Erin first stepped outside in the mornings, and she had to wake him.

Erin also hadn't been idle on the work front. The website advertising her services as a corporate image consultant was now completed and up and running. She knew that, because she checked it daily. Trouble was it had yet to bring in any enquiries, which was exactly what Spencer had predicted. That it was all very well setting up as a freelance, but that their industry relied on word-of-mouth recommendation and repeat business, and she'd find it impossible starting out in an area where no-one had ever heard of her.

Erin was determined to prove him wrong. She'd been planning for just this eventuality, so it was a case of putting those plans into action. Now that she was finding her feet domestically and practically, it was definitely time to concentrate on the professional side of her life. After all, what good was being an expert in enhancing a business's image, if she couldn't prove it by doing it to her own?

* * *

Dressed in jeans and a fleecy top, Erin had her head bent over a trowel when a voice floated over the front fence.

'Excuse me, but have you seen a twenty-something, sharp-suited, hot shot city executive anywhere?'

'Elaine!' Erin shrieked and leaped the picket fence to hug her sister. 'Why didn't you say you were coming? Oh, it's great to see you. It seems like ages!'

'I thought I'd surprise you. And it is ages. Couldn't you have gone off to find yourself somewhere a bit closer to home? I had to start out in the middle of the night!'

Erin leaned back and glanced over

her sister's shoulder.

'Where's everyone else?'

'I did what I threatened and parked them all with mum-in-law for twenty-four hours. She has her uses!' Elaine gazed at Owl Cottage properly for the first time. 'Hmm. I can see the attraction, I think.' She peered at Erin, her clothes and then her face. Finally, she nodded approvingly.

'It suits you here. Though I wouldn't have believed that.'

'Wouldn't you?' Erin picked up her sister's small overnight holdall. 'You never said anything.'

'No, but I thought it. Just like Spencer, I decided that you'd gone a bit mad,' Elaine said cheerfully.

'You never told me that, either.'

'Well, there's just something about that man that makes me want to take the opposite stand. Can't imagine why!'

Erin grinned. Elaine had never thought that Spencer was right for her, and had also never shied from letting her sister know.

'How does that saying go? About not understanding it, but defending to the death your right to do it!'

'Hopefully it won't come to that,' Erin cried.

Elaine tutted.

'What I'm trying to say is that it's a sister's prerogative to support her sibling to the hilt, even whilst privately thinking she's as mad as cheese!'

Laughing, Erin gave her another hug.

'I'm pleased you're here. There's so much to tell you, so much to show you!'

'I wouldn't mind seeing a pot of tea, and a chair.'

Elaine did look weary, Erin saw. And there was something different about her . . .

'You're pregnant again, aren't you?'

'Trust you to guess! I wanted to tell you, but never mind. Ah, that's better.' Elaine dropped on to the sofa and sighed before gazing around. 'This is quaint. Easy to keep clean?'

'Vacuumed top to bottom in eighteen

minutes, and without having to change sockets! Now, about the baby!'

'About that tea?' Elaine countered. 'And, yes, we're all thrilled, naturally. Perhaps you'll get a niece this time!'

'I don't mind which.' Erin was still taking in the news as she went through to put on the kettle.

'I do! A girl would even up the sides a bit. I'm outnumbered by boys at the moment. I do believe Graham's got his heart set on a cricket eleven! Fat chance, though — I've told him straight.'

Erin chuckled.

'When will we know?'

'My due date is November the fifth, of all days. Graham says if it is a girl we might have to call her Catherine.'

'Huh?'

'Catherine wheel!' Elaine's voice went quiet, then she suddenly gave a yelp which brought Erin rushing back in the room.

'It's a real cat!' Elaine was pointing at the window-sill. 'I thought it was an ornament until it moved!'

'That's Feather, my new lodger. She's decided that's her spot.'

Erin had to admit that the tortoiseshell cat looked more at home there than the rose-patterned jugs ever had.

Elaine was looking amused.

'You told me about the dopey cockerel. I'm looking forward to meeting him . . . I think. But a cat as well?'

'She was dumped on the doorstep a few days ago,' Erin explained. 'The woman who lived here used to take in strays, so perhaps someone thought the arrangement still stood.'

'And you've kept her anyway,' Elaine supplied as the cat tiptoed serenely over, looked up at her and gave a polite miaow. 'Yes, you may.'

To Erin's astonishment, Feather jumped up into Elaine's lap.

'There. Didn't know I spoke cat, did you? Actually neither did I!'

'She's never done that with me!' Erin marvelled.

Feather turned around twice and settled down in Elaine's lap, purring away.

'Pregnant females. Takes one to know one.'

Erin's hand went to her mouth.

'You don't think she's expecting, do you?'

Elaine shrugged, but gently so as not to disturb the cat.

'No idea. What do I know about felines?'

'What do I know about kittens?'

'I expect you'll learn when the time comes. She is a sweet cat, isn't she, for a waif and stray? And beautifully marked.' Her eyes widened eagerly. 'Talking of waifs and strays, did you ever find out what happened to your mystery man?'

'What mystery man?'

'What mystery man! You can't have forgotten that poor chap you mention just about every time we speak on the phone. The one who turned up looking for somewhere to rest his weary head, and you threw him back out into the stormy night.'

'Oh, him.' Erin placed a tea tray on the coffee table. 'I still have no idea what happened to him. Perhaps I dreamed him up! After all, I didn't realise I'd nodded off until the knocking at the door brought me to.'

'Then he can't have been a dream, idiot. You didn't meet him until after you woke up!'

'It's strange, though. No-one in the village seems to know who he is, not even Pete and Daph, and they know everyone. Mind you,' she added, 'there's not exactly a lot to go on. All I could give was a sketchy description, and I only spoke to him for a few minutes. But where did he come from, and where did he go?' Erin paused, stirring her tea. 'I did think of contacting the letting agent, but what possible excuse would I give for wanting to know? Except idle curiosity . . . ' She stopped, aware of her sister's amusement. 'What?'

'You. Pretending you didn't know who I was talking about. And as for idle curiosity, you've spent a lot of time thinking about him!'

Erin smiled, then gasped.

'I've just remembered I've got an appointment at two o'clock down at the village hall.'

The meeting she'd set up with two of the parish councillors was a first step towards building her business, by offering her services free of charge to promote the image of the village. Brundenham had its own website, which suggested it wanted to advance itself as a tourist destination. But Erin could see several ways in which it could be improved.

She picked up her phone.

'I'm going to rearrange the meeting now you're here.'

'Don't you dare,' Elaine scolded. 'I'd love to explore the village, the church and the little museum, And didn't you tell me there's a café, too? I can sit and wait in there until you've finished.'

* * *

Despite the sunshine it was chilly and Elaine, wrapped in a puffer coat and vivid striped scarf, was the only patron braving one of the steel tables outside the Rosy Leaf.

'I feel like a tourist!' She beamed up at a navy-suited Erin who'd come scuttling out of the village hall across the road in her high heels, a folder tucked under her arm.

It was the first time Erin had worn what she'd always thought of as normal clothes since leaving Manchester. It felt strange, like the first day back to work after a holiday.

'I'd better report to the council that my ideas are drawing people in already, then!' she joked. Then she shivered. 'Let's sit inside, shall we?'

'I've been watching those rooks up in the trees.' Elaine indicated across the road as she pushed back her chair. 'They're making nests, but how ever do they stay up there in this wind?'

'If they're Norfolk rooks then they've got used to it! It's the east wind that comes straight off the North Sea. The local people call it lazy,' Erin was saying as they entered the café, 'because instead of going round you, it goes straight through you!' She grinned, only half aware of a tall figure rising from a table at the back of the room.

Elaine was giving a sideways glance at the leaving customer, which caused Erin to sigh. Her sister always thought it was a discreet way of having a good gawp at someone without being obvious. Except it meant it was only too obvious to everyone else, and particularly to the person in question!

'Stop it!' she hissed, nudging Elaine in the elbow and turning to look up openly and smile at the man who was squeezing awkwardly past them in the café's narrow entrance way.

'Oh!' she blurted out. 'It's you!'

He glanced at them both, and she thought she caught a brief flicker of recognition in his blue-grey eyes. Then he dropped his gaze and squeezed on past to the door.

'It's him!' Erin exclaimed to Elaine.

She darted round to the front window to catch a glimpse of him passing by, but he must have gone the other way.

'Oh, blow it!' she said, much to the surprise of the couple seated at the window alcove table. 'Sorry,' she mumbled to them, and dashing back past a patiently amused Elaine, she wrenched open the door to the street.

His tall figure had just reached the corner, where he instantly disappeared from view.

'You sure you don't want to run after him?' Elaine pulled back two chairs at a vacant table.

'No, I'm certain it was him. I think I detected that slight limp again. Isn't it strange, though? We were only talking about him this morning.'

'You were. But I can see why. He's tasty, isn't he?'

'Mmm. Not in an obvious way, though.'

She looked at Elaine and they both burst into giggles.

'What's happening? We've reverted to teenagers again.'

'Well, I'm pregnant, so my hormones are naturally all over the place,' Elaine declared. 'What's your excuse?'

'Haven't got one.'

Elaine gave her a sceptical look.

'I haven't!' she insisted, plucking the menu from her sister's fingers. 'Have you chosen yet?'

'I'm going to go mad and have an éclair. What about you? It's my treat.'

Erin glanced disinterestedly through the list of pastries.

'Did I really talk a lot about him this morning?'

'Yep. And no doubt we'll be sitting up half the night talking about him, too!'

Erin put the menu face down on the table.

'I don't think I want anything to eat, thanks. Just tea for me today, please, Rosie,' she asked the woman in a rose-patterned apron who'd come to take their order.

Erin had met the owner, who ran the Rosy Leaf with her husband Oliver. She introduced her sister.

'That settles it,' Elaine said, sitting back with a satisfied expression after Rosie had disappeared though the back. 'It's love. The only other time I've ever known you to lose your appetite is when we came out of 'Enemy At The Gates', and you'd fallen in love with Jude Law!'

Back at Owl Cottage, Elaine explored the back garden and had a meeting with Napoleon while Erin prepared some food for later.

'Good job Napoleon gets on with the cat!' Elaine called through the open kitchen window.

'There was a bit of bad language on both sides the first day, but then they called a truce and decided to ignore each other, thank goodness.'

After supper, the conversation got round to Spencer who, Elaine pointed out, despite being good-looking in a very obvious way, had never once put

Erin off her food.

'Yes, but I'm still disappointed that he's not got in touch. Well, he has,' she immediately corrected herself. 'He called a couple of times, actually.'

'You never said.'

'Nothing to tell. They only lasted a few minutes each. He sounded very brisk, very impersonal.'

'What did he say?'

'He just apologised for having to call me, but he had queries about a couple of the clients I used to deal with.'

Elaine sat back. Her cheeks looked very red.

'It's the woodburner,' Erin told her. 'It really throws out the heat. If you get up a minute, I'll move back the sofa.'

'Where to, the garden? I wasn't huffing and puffing at the woodburner, anyway. It's lovely. I'm wondering if Graham would be up for us having one put in. And I wouldn't mind one of these about the house, as well.' She stroked Feather's silky fur lovingly.

'The feeling seems to be mutual.'

'The boys would love a pet. If she does have kittens, you will let me know?'

'Yes, but if you go home with talk of cats, Graham will think I've had a really bad influence on you.'

'He knows that already!'

They made faces, then smiled at each other fondly.

'Why were you huffing and puffing, then? About Spencer?'

'No. At you, Erin! You can't be so naïve as to believe he was calling you up about some client details. Don't you think he's got all that information at his fingertips?'

'I did wonder.'

'He thought you'd hear the sound of his voice and go all weak-kneed, saying you'd made the biggest mistake of your life and asking how soon could he come and pick you up?'

'Huh! Knowing Spencer, he'd expect me to make my own way there!'

But she knew Elaine was right. Things had been left unsatisfactorily between her and Spencer, mainly because he'd refused to accept that she wouldn't be back within a matter of weeks with her tail between her legs.

She sighed.

'I just wish I knew where we stood.'

In the month that Erin had been in Brundenham she'd had plenty of time and distance to explore her feelings over Spencer, and one thing was certain. She'd hardly missed him, and she hadn't missed their hectic lifestyle one bit.

A couple of days after Elaine's visit, Erin got another call from her old office, this time from a female colleague. It started as a supposed query, but very soon Wendy got on to the real point, which was to let Erin know that she'd been replaced. Spencer had appointed a new executive consultant with a long and impressive list of past client testimonials to her credit.

Bully for her, Erin thought uncharitably as Wendy droned on.

Then her ears really pricked up.

41

' . . . Spencer was seen taking her into Dove's yesterday evening for dinner.'

Erin made an excuse about a call on another line, and put down the phone. Dove's. Ouch, that stung! It had been their favourite restaurant on special occasions.

'Well, Feather,' she told the cat, who was rubbing round her ankles in the hope of a mid-morning snack, 'he's moving on with his life. And that's what we're going to do, too, aren't we?'

She bent lower. The cat's girth was definitely larger. But was it pregnancy, or her fondness for tinned sardines?

★ ★ ★

Erin was feeling more at home in Brundenham every day. She shopped locally as much as possible. The village was lucky in still having a convenience store, with a post-office counter that opened three days a week. The museum was fascinating, being housed in what once had been the village lock-up. All Saints' church was impressively large, the original 12th-century structure having been extended with donations from landowners made wealthy from the wool trade. She learned this from a leaflet and from a volunteer whom she'd found dusting inside.

'We like to keep the church open daily from Easter to Harvest Festival, if we can. It depends if we get enough people prepared to commit to daily unlocking and locking up again, for a week at a time.'

The woman had introduced herself as Anne Grange. They chatted some more, and Erin came away with her name on the key holder rota for a week's duty in July and again in late August.

Anne had been very grateful.

'So many of our regulars are away on holiday then.'

Erin hadn't given a thought to summer holidays. Being in Brundenham was like being on permanent holiday! And Owl Cottage was like a holiday home.

Whoever owned this was a very lucky person, yet she almost felt sorry for them, too. By not having the pleasure of living here, they were missing something very special.

If her love-life seemed set on a slippery downwards incline, at least Erin's professional plans were on more of an even course. Her work with the parish councillors on a more tourist-focused image for the village was moving forwards, albeit at a snail-like pace. She'd been invited to speak a few words at the next meeting, but that wouldn't be until the last Thursday in the month.

In the meantime, she was casting her net wider by checking out all the local businesses with a view to offering her services. This had already borne results, and her diary had two other appointments pencilled in — one with the owner of a small gym and fitness club, the other with the manager of a garden centre. It was slow progress, but as she kept reminding herself, she'd known it wasn't going to be easy starting from scratch.

She had budgeted her finances very carefully before embarking on her leap year, so she knew she had enough in the bank to survive at least that long. Which was just as well because, if Wendy's piece of gossip was true, she couldn't run back to Spencer any time soon and expect to get her old life back . . . even if she wanted to.

It was the following afternoon, and Erin had been for a quick walk that had ended up taking longer than expected. It was amazing how often she bumped into the same people, dog-walkers mainly. Nearly everyone stopped for a few words, even if it was only about the weather.

Several people asked if she intended getting a dog. She would have loved one, but it was the uncertainty of her future that stopped her. It was bad enough worrying about Feather and Feather's kittens, if or when they came. Feather might have to go to an animal shelter.

Erin found herself recoiling at the thought. No, wherever she ended up after her year in Brundenham, Feather would stay with her. She would settle in a flat.

Erin didn't know if she could again, though. She loved her garden. The lettuce and the carrot seeds were just coming up, and the first potato leaves had started to poke through the soil. They'd need earthing up, Pete told her, to avoid frost damage. That would be a job for this weekend.

With her thoughts on gardening plans as she turned into the lane, Erin was nearly on top of the strange Silver Audi parked outside Owl Cottage before she noticed it. She stopped dead as Spencer sprang out of the driver's side. He looked fresh, uncrumpled and as attractive as ever.

'What do you say?' he said with a smile.

Her mind had gone blank.

'You've got a new car,' she said eventually.

'Yes.' He gave a short laugh. 'Like it?'

'It's great,' she said, almost automatically. Spencer was a real car snob. 'Puts mine in the shade.'

'Is that yours?' he asked, and pointed to the rather less impressive sky-blue vehicle he'd parked behind.

She nodded. She'd discovered in her first week that a car was essential in the country. Pete Carr had put her on to a local second-hand car dealer who said he'd be happy to take the motor back in a year's time.

'Yep. It's cheap to run, rather temperamental, but gets me from A to B. Most of the time,' she added.

Actually, she'd grown rather fond of Metal Mickey, as she'd come to call him.

She suddenly felt awkward.

'I'm not sure why we're discussing cars.'

'Because we're putting off the moment when I ask you if you've come to your senses yet?'

She knew he was only half joking. There'd always been a tiny trace of old-fashioned chauvinism in Spencer.

Nothing overt or specific, and definitely not in the workplace. It was only in their personal relationship that she'd ever sensed it; an impression that he expected to be the principal decision-maker. Or perhaps he was just bossy!

Inside the cottage Erin deliberately busied herself with hanging up her jacket so she wouldn't have to see Spencer's response to the cramped, slightly chaotic interior.

'Coffee?' she said briskly, heading for the kitchen.

'OK.' He followed her through, and watched while she tried to fill the kettle.

'There's a door there, if you want to see the back garden properly.'

'No, thanks.' He turned away from the window. 'I'm really not the outdoorsy type.'

No, he definitely wasn't. Back in the living-room he perched on the edge of the small sofa and she couldn't help noticing how out of place he seemed there, too. It wasn't just the sharply-tailored suit, nor the shiny Italian leather shoes. Mainly it was his obvious discomfort in this environment.

Spencer had laughed when she'd first suggested a move to the country, to run the business jointly from there. When he'd realised she was serious, he had simply refused to consider it. She'd thought at the time how obstinate he was, not to even give her idea a fair hearing.

But he'd been right to dismiss it, she could see that now. If she'd harboured any lingering hope that he might still be prepared to give it a try, his presence here surely closed the book on that for good.

What she'd done had been the right course of action for her. The best thing would be for them to end their relationship. But Spencer took the wind out of her sails by suddenly reaching out for her hand and drawing her to sit down beside him.

'Look, Erin, I sort of see what the attraction is here. But I honestly can't see how this is going to pan out for you?'

'It's panning out already, thank you very much.' She pulled her hand away. 'I've got several leads, and one client in the bag already.' A bit of poetic licence where the parish council was concerned, but Erin felt justified.

'I don't doubt your ability, Erin, you know that. But starting from scratch like this . . . '

'It's going to take time, of course. I've given myself a whole year.'

'Two months have gone already.'

'Yes.' She turned towards him again. 'And it's taken that long for you to come and see me.'

His eyes searched her face.

'I miss you,' he said, but his tone was bland, emotionless. 'I can't live without you. I should never have let you go. There, now I've admitted it, are you happy? Now will you come back?'

She stared at him in disbelief. All through her resignation she'd felt that Spencer was waiting for her to admit she'd made a mistake, and that she wouldn't go through with it.

But she had, and she was proud of such perseverance in the face of his negativity. She'd found Owl Cottage, sub-let her apartment, cleared her desk and said goodbye.

She squared her shoulders and faced him.

'If you truly miss me, then I'm sorry, Spencer, really I am. But I'm not going back to how we were.' She took a deep breath. 'I admit that I did once think we had might have had a future together as a couple . . . '

'We did!' he interrupted crossly. 'We still do, don't we?'

Biting her lip, she shook her head.

'We want different things.'

'We were fine with what we had.'

'But we weren't going anywhere.'

'Because there was nothing wrong with things as they were!' Spencer snapped, standing up. 'We're just going around in circles.'

'We should have talked all this through before I left,' she murmured, turning away.

'I didn't think there was any need.' He caught her arm and pulled her back to face him.

'I've had time to think. Our mistake was to mix business with a personal relationship. What about if you came back, but not to work for me?'

Erin could see where this was leading.

'I heard you'd found a replacement for me.'

'Ah, the office jungle drums. That was quick!' He scowled briefly. 'But, Erin, I mean it about you and me. If you were to come back to Manchester . . .'

'I've sub-let my flat.'

'We could find a place together?'

The expression on her face must have told him her answer.

'I shouldn't have bothered coming.' Spencer strode off towards his car. On the point of dipping to get in, he stopped and looked back at her. 'You know where I am if you want to get in touch.'

May Meetings

Erin gave a loud whoop when she opened her e-mails and found her website had its first proper enquiry.

After reading the message from James Standing, General Manager for Greensides Hotel, she immediately Googled the place. It was a 25-bedroomed establishment just over the other side of Brundenham. She telephoned to make an appointment with Mr Standing.

'Jim's somewhere or other,' came the casually friendly voice down the line. 'Hang on a sec and I'll put you through to Brad.'

'Brad' announced himself rather stiffly as Bradley Cavill, Accounts Manager. He, it turned out, had access to the general manager's diary. A day and time was fixed.

'There, Feather, what do you think of that?' She crossed over to the alcove at the side of the fireplace.

Feather was suckling three kittens — two tortoiseshell, like herself, and one ginger — and was purring like a steam engine. Erin's heart melted every time she looked at them. Nearly three weeks old, their eyes had opened now, and when they weren't eating or sleeping they were just starting to explore their environment.

She'd already erected a wire run in the garden so they could play outside on the grass in safety. What Napoleon would make of that would be interesting. The day the fence went up, the cockerel had stalked all the way round the frame, crowing with a proprietorial air.

*   *   *

The very next afternoon, dressed casually in cream trousers and a multi-coloured top, she climbed into Metal Mickey and headed for Greensides.

The May countryside was looking gorgeous. Ornamental cherry trees lined the roads like sticks of pink and white candyfloss. Beyond the burgeoning hedgerows that were thick with hawthorn and elder blossoms, she had glimpses of fields that were turning greener every day.

She easily found a space in the large car park and walked into Reception. There were two women on duty behind the desk, both dark-haired, one slightly older with an immaculately shaped bob, the younger sporting a mass of unruly curls. It was the more elegant receptionist who came forwards immediately, appraising Erin with a cool gaze.

'May I help you?'

'Do you serve afternoon tea to non-residents?'

'Certainly, madam. If you'd like to take a seat . . . ' She indicated over Erin's shoulder to an informal seating area comprising comfortable-looking, tan leather chairs and sofas and a couple of occasional tables scattered with magazines ' . . . I'll have a tray brought to you.'

'Thank you,' Erin said, but the woman had already turned away to return to the desk. As she picked up the phone, her younger colleague looked up.

'No need to buzz the kitchen, Cheryl. I'm heading that way now.'

Erin recognised the voice from her call the day before. The girl passed through a door that led to the back regions.

Erin chose a chair at right angles to the desk, so that she could have a good view of both the reception area and the view from the window at the side of the hotel. There was a broad terrace outside which, with a few tables and chairs and some decorative planting, could easily be turned into a lovely casual eating area with a pleasant view.

As she waited, flicking through a magazine, she kept one ear on the conversations at Reception. It wasn't a terribly busy day. A family of four was checked out with razor-sharp efficiency.

A couple of phone calls came in. They both seemed to be enquiries about room availability, and again Cheryl dealt with them with capable crispness.

It was the younger, more ebullient receptionist who brought out the tea.

'There you go.' She smiled, plonking down the tray. 'If you need more hot water, just yell out.'

'Thank you.'

Instead of leaving, the girl hovered.

'So, visiting the area on holiday, are you?'

'No, I've only recently moved to Norfolk.'

'From 'oop north', aren't you?'

Erin was surprised. She knew she had a trace of Mancunian, but hadn't thought it was that pronounced.

The first receptionist materialised at the girl's arm.

'Do you have a moment, Claire?'

Claire followed Cheryl back to the desk. Their conversation continued out of earshot, but Erin could guess that Claire was getting a dressing-down.

The tea was good and hot. Erin drained her cup and bent down to pick up her bag and dig out her purse to pay. She heard the footsteps of a new arrival, but by the time she looked up the figure had crossed the foyer and disappeared through a door. The impression Erin had was fleeting, but she was almost certain it was him. Mystery Man!

As she walked over to the reception desk she took several glances in that direction, but the heavy swing fire door he'd gone through was closed, and there was no sign or any other clue of whether it was public or private quarters beyond it.

Claire came forwards with a beaming smile.

'I hope your tea was OK.' She broke off to speak over her shoulder to Cheryl. 'He's just come back in, I've seen him go through.'

Who? Erin itched to ask. She was tantalisingly close to discovering Mystery Man's name, at least. She found herself holding her breath for Cheryl's response.

'Thank you,' Cheryl said tightly.

She tip-tapped across the foyer in a pair of sensibly heeled, navy court shoes.

'There you go.' Claire handed out Erin's change. 'P'raps we'll see you back again?'

'Pardon? Oh, yes.' Erin felt herself flush, not wanting to quite meet Claire's open face.

They would be seeing her again on Friday afternoon in her professional capacity. Today's kind of visit did sometimes make her feel guilty, but there was no substitute for gaining valuable first-hand impressions of an organisation.

On the return journey, the country-side views were pushed to the periphery of Erin's mind. She was already focusing on Greensides and the ways in which she could help improve its image. By Friday's meeting she would have drawn up some initial proposals to present to Mr Standing.

Elaine phoned that evening. Erin told her about the fleeting suspected sighting at Greensides.

'Intriguing. Do you think he might be staying there?'

'That's what I wondered. An expensive alternative to renting, though!'

'You should have followed him, Erin.'

'Yes, that would have looked good, wouldn't it? Chasing a man through the hotel! Very professional when I go back to see them on Friday. It feels awkward enough as it is.'

Elaine gave a gasp.

'I've just thought — he could be a member of staff. He could even be the manager bloke you're meeting!'

'Do you think I haven't thought of that? But I doubt it. He was wearing casual trousers and a shirt with the sleeves rolled up.'

'I guess.' Elaine sounded disappointed. 'Never mind. Keep me posted. How's my kitten coming along?'

Erin looked across at the trio, fast

asleep in the basket. Every so often they stretched and murmured. Feather, who'd adopted an air of smugness since giving birth, was taking the opportunity of some time-out. She was back in her old, favoured spot on the front window-sill and giving herself a comprehensive all-over wash.

'They're all fine. I can't believe how big they're grown in three weeks!'

Thank goodness Daph had come straight round the evening Feather gave birth, if only to reassure Erin that everything was proceeding as it should.

And as Daph had pointed out, 'Feather's more than up to the task. It's likely she's had kittens before.'

Erin had already made enquiries with the veterinary practice in Brundenham to have her spayed, so this litter would be the cat's last.

With Daph's married daughter, Karen, wanting one kitten, and Elaine putting claim to another, that only left one for which to find a home. The smallest kitten, the gingery-brown female one that Erin had called Mouse.

'A mistake to name it,' Daph had scolded, her head on one side, 'if you're intending to let it go.'

*　*　*

It was just Cheryl on duty when Erin returned to Greensides. This time Erin was dressed in one of her business outfits — a tailored cream trouser suit — and her hair was coiled up and neatly pinned. She felt sure Cheryl remembered her from two days earlier, yet the receptionist gave no sign they'd ever met or spoken before.

Again she was directed over to the seating area, and was told that Mr Standing would be informed she had arrived.

Erin fiddled with her briefcase in between taking rapid glances every time she heard a door open or a footstep fall. Her mouth felt dry. She told herself there was no need for nerves, that a meeting with a prospective client was an everyday event. Except that this was the most important one she'd faced in the last three months, and added to the mix was the niggling speculation that Mr Standing might actually turn out to be Mystery Man.

He wasn't. There was a tiny bit of disappointment, but it was predominantly relief that surged through Erin's body when a comfortably-built man of about forty-five strode across the foyer with his hand outstretched.

'Miss Mallowson! Sorry to keep you waiting.'

She smiled back, standing up and taking his hand.

'Please, call me Erin.'

'Jim,' he reciprocated. 'My office is this way. Would you like some coffee?'

'Please.'

'Cheryl, would you mind rustling us up some coffee?' Jim indicated Erin towards the door that Mystery Man had gone through a few days before. So that was the staff area of the premises!

Jim Standing's office was the first room off a narrow corridor, and overlooked the same view that Erin had admired from Reception.

'The golf course starts on the other side of our boundaries,' he explained, following her line of sight before pulling out a chair for her. 'It's our main selling point. A lot of our customers stay here primarily for the golfing. But there are several other hotels, motels and guest houses in a ten-mile radius, so we've healthy competition.'

She'd already gathered that from her research.

'You've a big advantage by being within walking distance of the golf course. There's also a lot of other local activities and amenities that could bring in more business.'

She went on to outline some of the marketing approaches and strategies that she felt could benefit Greensides. When she'd finished, Jim Standing was nodding.

They were interrupted by a polite tap at the door. Cheryl brought in a tray of coffee and placed it on the desk. Jim thanked her, and she left as crisply as she'd entered.

That reminded Erin of another important area which might benefit from change.

'Apart from the marketing side, there are other initiatives which could be taken, involving staff and training.' She paused. This was often the most delicate area to tackle. 'I did pop in for tea the other afternoon, just to get an impartial feel of the business.'

'Ah. Reception,' Jim Standing said, with an expression that suggested he knew where Erin was going next.

'We both know it's the first impression of a business, and in the hotel business it's also the last. Yours is good, but I feel, with a few tweaks, it could be excellent.'

'I like what I'm hearing so far, Erin. If we employed your services, what sort of fee would be talking about?'

With the deal almost fixed, Erin felt herself begin to relax. Over coffee, they discussed and arrived at a fee.

'Right, Erin, when can you make a start?'

'How about right now?'

Jim Standing was surprised but agreeable.

'Wonderful! Oh, excuse me . . . ' The phone on his desk began to ring, and he picked it up.

'I'll come straight down. Thanks. Slight hitch in the kitchen,' he explained, replacing the receiver. 'I'll be as quick as I can.'

She'd already returned the sheets of notes to her briefcase, and stood waiting just by the door.

'Actually, before you go, Jim, would it be possible to see a breakdown of guest numbers? It'd be useful to know the proportion of repeat visitors, if you keep that information.'

'My new accounts manager should have all those figures at his fingertips. I'll show you to his office.'

It was a short walk to the room next door.

'Brad, this is Erin Mallowson.'

Erin had completely forgotten about Mystery Man . . . until she looked up into the cool blue-grey eyes of the tall, fair-haired man that was Brad Cavill.

It was the first proper chance she'd had to see him in full light. Her heart started to beat wildly. She saw his look of recognition, as he must have seen hers.

He repositioned a spare chair from the wall to rest next to his and invited her to sit down.

She proceeded to tell him why Jim had called her in, and how she proposed to tackle the areas she'd highlighted.

Brad summoned up the exact information she required, and as they peered at the figures on the screen their shoulders almost brushed. She could smell the pine-forest tang of his aftershave.

'This is useful,' she said. 'May I take a copy with me?'

'Sure.'

He went over to switch on the printer

and her eyes followed the back of his head. She noticed how the ends of his hair just started to curl around his well-shaped ears.

'Won't take a second to warm up,' he said.

Brad Cavill's fingers were drumming the plastic casing of the printer. Impatient, or was he eager to be rid of her?

'Would you like some coffee?' he asked out of the blue.

'Thanks, but no. I had some with Jim earlier. Oh, there we are.'

The printer finally stuttered into life and began spewing out sheets. She wasn't sure whether to be relieved that the awkward moments were finally over, or annoyed at wasting an opportunity to find out more about him.

With the sheaf of accounts print-outs tucked inside her file, Erin stood up.

'Thanks, Brad. These are exactly what I need to take back home and analyse. If you wouldn't mind telling Jim I'll be in touch in a day or two?'

Brad, too, stood up and nodded.

'If you need any more info, just give me a bell. I can e-mail anything over to you.'

He hadn't been effusively friendly, but he was helpful, well-organised and clearly on top of his job. And Jim had said he was new, too. Impressive.

If he'd not long had this job, it probably explained why he'd been looking for somewhere local to live. She took a quick breath and smiled up at him as she held out her hand.

'It's nice to meet you properly at last.'

He took her hand in a brief shake.

'You, too.' He paused, then asked rather awkwardly, 'You're settling in to Brundenham, OK?'

'Yes, it's a lovely village. I'd never even heard of it before I came here.'

She thought she'd better not mention Owl Cottage in case it was still a sore point. She itched to ask if he'd found an alternative, but didn't dare in case he hadn't.

When they reached Reception, Erin assumed he'd leave her there. Claire was on duty behind the desk now. Her eyes widened expressively when she recognised Erin.

'Hi, again! I've just heard who you are. I told Cheryl you were no ordinary customer when you came in last time.'

'I dropped in for tea the other afternoon,' Erin explained to Brad. 'It's nice to see you again, Claire. I'll probably be around the hotel now and then over the next few weeks.'

'And I'm just going to lunch,' Brad told Claire. 'If you wouldn't mind taking any messages?'

'Course not, Brad. Have a nice time, you two,' she called, a hint of playfulness in her voice.

Erin made her way to her car, Brad continuing to walk by her side. He did have a tiny trace of a limp, though it was barely detectable.

'Is there a car park for staff cars?' she asked, stopping at Metal Mickey and fishing for her keys.

'Yes, behind the hotel, but there's usually space in the main car park, so you'll be OK to use it any time you come over.'

'Right.' It wasn't really what she meant.

'Be seeing you, then.'

As Brad set off in the direction of the main drive towards the gates, it suddenly occurred to Erin that he might not own a car at all.

'I'm going back through the village if you're going that way and would like a lift?' she called.

He stopped and turned.

'Oh.' He sounded slightly surprised. 'Yes, if you're sure. Thanks very much.' He retraced his steps back to her.

She unlocked the passenger door. The car had been sitting in the sun for over an hour, and it was like climbing into an oven. She quickly wound down the windows.

'No air-conditioning, I'm afraid,' she apologised, thinking how horrified Spencer would be. 'I think this car was built before it was invented!'

'There will be a breeze when we get moving,' he remarked. 'Nature's own air-conditioning.'

Erin liked that.

Pulling out from the drive on to the main road gave her the opportunity to sneak yet another look at him. Just as she was thinking what a reserved, private sort of person he was, he caught her looking and broke into a smile. It transformed his face.

At the risk of ruining the change of atmosphere, she couldn't resist asking if he'd found somewhere else to rent.

'Nothing suitable in the village in my price range,' he said. 'There's a bedsit above the Rosy Leaf, but that doesn't have a garden, unfortunately.'

'And is a garden important?'

'I have a dog. He's with my sister at the moment, but I'd like to get settled somewhere where I can have him back with me.'

'And Owl Cottage would have been ideal,' she murmured.

'I'm sorry if I sounded sharp that night I turned up.'

'Don't be. I could see you were disappointed.'

'There'd been a mix-up at the agents. You'd spoken to one partner, I'd spoken to another. But they'd not spoken to each other! Just unfortunate.' He shrugged.

Erin was confused. That slightly fatalistic air had come down on him again.

'Well, I hope something suitable turns up again soon,' she said, swinging the car into the village's main street. 'If all else fails, Owl Cottage should be up for rent again in nine months time. I've only signed a year's lease on it.'

'Oh?' He turned towards her. 'What then?'

She'd already told him, hadn't she?

'The cottage will probably be available again next March, if the owner wants to continue renting it out.'

'No, I meant for you, Erin.'

'Oh. I'm not sure,' she admitted

hesitantly. 'Depends how the year works out.'

'Don't you mind?' he asked. 'Not knowing? Not having a plan for after that?'

She blinked at him, the realisation suddenly hitting with full force for the first time. What her action was telling her now, with a benefit of a few months' hindsight, was just how desperate she'd been to swap her old life for something else.

'It is a bit of a leap into the unknown for me,' she admitted lightly after realising Brad was still patiently waiting for a response. 'It might be fun, though, just seeing where life takes me from now on.'

'Oh,' Brad said, which effectively told her nothing about what he thought of that.

Erin pulled up in the village hall car park but left the engine running. Brad unclipped his seat belt.

'Thanks for the lift, Erin. I enjoy the walks to and from the village, but sometimes it's a rush to get there and back in an hour.'

'Well, I expect Jim Standing wouldn't mind if you took a bit longer and worked a bit later to make it up.'

'You're right. He's a decent sort. But I don't want to take advantage. I've only recently started at Greensides. It's my first job since qualifying as an accountant. It took me a while to find it, and took me out of my area, too. I was in Essex before,' he explained.

'So where are you living now, then?'

'At Greensides. In one of the staff rooms. It means I've no excuse for getting in late! But they're for the shift workers really, so it's not ideal.'

'No,' she agreed thoughtfully. 'I'll keep my nose to the ground, Brad, and if I hear of anything going, I'll let you know.'

'Thanks,' he said. 'Be seeing you back at Greensides in the near future, then.' He smiled briefly, got out of the car and closed the door, which promptly swung back open.

'It needs a good whack,' she advised with a grin. 'More than that . . . there, that's done it!'

On the third attempt he'd finally given it enough of a shove to secure it. Erin gave a wave of her hand as she pulled away.

Brad Cavill, Accounts Manager and live-in employee of Greensides Hotel. She had a quite a lot to tell Elaine now. His name, occupation, where he was living and where he came from, and that he had a dog.

But the core of the man remained a mystery . . .

June Date

For the next while Greensides Hotel became a familiar place to Erin. She'd made several more visits, fostered relationships with the local media for positive Press coverage and instigated training for the front-of-house staff. She'd fleetingly considered asking Spencer to come over and give a session but she'd quickly dismissed the idea, and had instead engaged a very good freelance staff trainer she'd worked with in the past.

She'd also had a couple of meetings with Brad, who was in charge of updating the hotel's rather dusty website and setting up Twitter and Facebook accounts, to spread the word on late-room availability and special deals and to advertise upcoming functions. The results of all these efforts were beginning to show. There were increased bookings, and a real buzz and energy about the hotel.

An added bonus was that working with Greensides had brought in other enquiries, and Erin was now advising two other companies who were employing her services.

Owl Cottage was also a busy place. At last, Erin's experiments with interior design were beginning to pay off, and the rooms had taken on the countrified look.

By midsummer, Feather's kittens were old enough to leave home. Daph came round with a pet basket to take away the one promised to her daughter, Karen.

'Sorry, Feather.' Daph plucked up one of the two boy kittens. She held it up in the air, where it reached out and batted Daph on the head. 'Hey, you! Tyson, that would be a good name for you. I might suggest it to Karen.'

'I think Feather will be grateful for a bit of peace and quiet.' Erin smiled, nodding at the mother cat, who sat placidly watching proceedings at a distance. 'Bye, bye, Tyson.' She stroked the kitten's head. 'Enjoy your new home.'

'If I know my daughter, he'll be spoiled rotten,' Daph said. 'When's your sister taking the other one?'

'Not for another month. They're coming over when the school breaks up. It's the end of my nephew William's first year at grown-up school. Jamie starts there in September.'

'That's such an exciting time,' Daph remarked, dewy-eyed. 'It only seems like five minutes ago since I was taking my two up the lane to the school, and now look at them. Karen married with a toddler of her own, and Kevin with his new starter flat. Pity it's right in Norwich, though.' She caught Erin's eye and gave an embarrassed laugh. 'Listen to me. It's only twenty-five minutes away, door to door. I make it sound like the other side of the world!'

'And Pete's in and out of Norwich quite often, isn't he?'

Daph nodded.

'Especially now the university's breaking up. Still, I bet you can't wait to spend some time with your family again,'

'Yes, it feels like ages.'

'New kitten, then new baby on the way. Your Elaine's going to be busy.'

'I know.' Erin gave a little sigh. 'If I'd known she was going to get herself pregnant again, I might have thought twice about moving so far away.'

'Still, it's done and you're here now. Pete was only saying the other day that you're looking quite different from the day you moved in.'

Erin was surprised.

'Am I? Yeah, I suppose I am.' She certainly felt different, healthier and happier. 'I'm definitely less stressed. Well, still a bit stressed, but in a different way.'

'You're mistress of your own destiny now, aren't you?' Daph looked surprised at her own words and spluttered with laughter. 'That's a bit poetic for me!'

'But I know what you mean, Daph, and you're right. When you're working for yourself, you've only got yourself to blame if you sink or swim.'

'That's Pete's philosophy exactly. He might not bring in a fortune, him and his van, but he's happy being a one-man band. Oh, which reminds me.' Daph's eyes widened. 'He's got a surprise for you.'

'Really?'

'No, I won't spoil it, but I'll give you a clue,' Daph said delightedly, as she picked up with the basket containing Tyson. 'One out, half a dozen in.'

That was cryptic. Erin hoped she didn't mean more cats.

After Daph had gone, Erin sat down to work on some ideas for one of the new clients, and then the phone rang.

'Hello? It's Brad here. Brad Cavill.'

She'd recognised his voice as soon as he'd said hello. Although still a bit of a mystery man, he was unbending a little more each time they met. But then, each time they met was on business, so chit-chat never really came into it all that much. Or not as much as Erin would have liked.

He'd never had occasion to ring her

before. Although she'd entertained the occasional flight of fancy that he might ask to see her outside of work, she could only assume he was calling about business now.

'Hi, Brad. Is there a problem?'

'Um . . . ' There was a slight pause that suggested the reason wasn't work related after all. Erin found herself holding her breath.

'No, I was just wondering if, um . . . '

'What?' she wanted to yell.

'You remember I mentioned that vacant bedsit above the Rosy Leaf? Well, I've decided to take it.'

'Oh.'

It was a bit of a surprise, but the last time they'd mentioned accommodation, she'd got the impression that he'd had enough of living in staff quarters.

'Good for you, Brad. I know it's not ideal. No outside space for your dog.'

'No, but at least it'll give me a bit more independence.'

'Oh, yes.' She could definitely identify with that. She was still wondering why he'd called her up, though. 'So when you do you move in?'

'This weekend.'

'Great, if you need any help, just ask.'

'I've not got very much stuff, but I was wondering if you knew of anyone with a small van?'

Immediately she thought of Pete. But then again, it was such a small job, and she was sure Pete wouldn't mind.

'I could help.' Eventually she was able to convince Brad that it would be no trouble, and that she and Mickey would turn up at Greensides at ten o'clock sharp on Saturday morning.

★　★　★

'It's a lovely little place,' she remarked, after inspecting the rooms above the café.

And it was, with its gnarled beams and wonky floors and tiny-paned windows overlooking the main street.

'Yes, it is, isn't it? I think I knew that, but it's nice to have a second opinion.'

He looked at her, and Erin, who'd been on the point of replying, stopped. There was something in the warmth of that look which signalled a subtle change. She'd long since figured he was a man who didn't find it easy to express his feelings, that it took him time to trust new people.

Dare she believe that point had now been reached between them?

'Erin . . . ' He moved a step closer.

'Coo-eee,' a voice sang out, accompanied by light footsteps on the stairs. 'Just wanted to make sure our tenant is settling in!'

It was Rosie, who together with her husband Oliver ran the café and owned the building that comprised the ground floor business and the upstairs accommodation.

Rosie seemed only slightly surprised to see Erin, whom she recognised from her visits to the café.

'Hello again, love. I didn't know you were a friend of Brad's. But then, why would I?'

84

Erin shared a quick look with Brad. Did he think of her as a friend, too? She hoped so.

'Now, Brad, you sure you can live with the café opening up Friday and Saturday evenings?'

It was a newish venture, she explained, when for two nights a week, the Rosy Leaf would be transformed into Rosie's Bistro.

Brad assured her it was fine with him.

'I can't see any of my mainly retired clientele getting rowdy and disturbing you.' She grinned. 'Most of the youngsters in the village shoot off into Norwich for the weekend nightlife.'

Brad glanced at Erin with a bright look in his eyes, the significance of which she couldn't quite grasp, before turning to Rosie.

'Does that mean we wouldn't qualify for a table, then?'

'Whenever you want one, Brad. Just say the word.'

Again Brad glanced at Erin, this time

with questioning expression. She found herself nodding.

'Any chance of a table for two tonight?'

'You're on.' Rosie smiled at him before heading back down the stairs. 'Eight o'clock OK?'

The second she'd gone, doubt clouded Brad's face.

'Sorry, Erin, I steam-rollered you into that. I didn't even ask if you were free, let alone if you wanted to!'

Erin nodded.

'Yes, I am, and yes, I'd love to.'

In fact, she thought to herself as she made her way back home, she was beginning to think he'd never ask!

* * *

She couldn't wait to hear what Elaine would make of the development, but decided, rather than call her straight away, she'd hold fire until after the dinner date. Which was just as well, because when she got back Pete Carr was waiting outside Owl Cottage. He'd brought her a surprise.

'Chickens?' she exclaimed, watching Pete unpack four russet-feathered hens from a crate.

Napoleon was equally surprised and equally delighted. He strutted round them with a wicked look in his eye.

'If he had a moustache he'd be twirling it!' Pete laughed, watching. 'Now, these girls are about five months old, so they should start laying any day now. You'll be self-sufficient in eggs, at least.'

She made Pete a mug of tea and a sandwich, and worked on one of her new accounts while he set to in the garden, niftily setting up a wire-netting-enclosed run at the side of the garden shed. After cutting through a hole for access, he fixed a perch for roosting and, turning the crate on its side, transformed it into a nest box.

'You've done this before.' Erin smiled.

He nodded.

'We've always kept a few chooks in the garden, ever since the kids were little. Nice creatures, hens. Very relaxing.'

And they were, she discovered after Pete had gone, as she sat on the wooden bench and watched the new girls peck around in the soil and grass for insects.

She'd have to give them all names, ones suitably regal as consorts of Napoleon. Josephine, obviously. And hadn't he got married again? To . . .

She dredged her rusty history brain cells. Marie Louise, was it? Yes, that sounded right. She was a bit stuck after her, but then recalled an old film that had been on one Sunday afternoon, called Desirée, about a girl who'd fallen for the Emperor's charms.

Now she really had run out.

'You'll just have be Number Four, I'm afraid, until inspiration strikes.' Except they all looked identical, so she no idea which was which anyway! She burst out laughing, and they all stopped

88

pecking to stare up her, blinking. It felt wonderfully peaceful, sitting in the sunshine and talking to chickens. Erin stretched out her arms and legs, feeling free and relaxed and incredibly fortunate with her lot.

Suddenly she realised it was nearly seven, and she had to shoot inside and start getting ready for her date with Brad.

She changed several times. Initially she put on her most expensive dress. It was a designer number in dark navy chiffon with elaborate ruffles. She'd only worn it once before, at an industry awards dinner, and it had drawn many compliments on the night. But it didn't feel right for her date with Brad, somehow. Eventually she chose a simpler shift dress, in cream linen with a tiny flower motif. She'd always felt comfortable and very feminine in it.

Rosie's practical plastic-topped tables had been covered with jaunty red gingham cloths, each one illuminated by a candle in a rustic bottle, and decorated with a little posy of real flowers. Slightly corny, but they created just the right sort of atmosphere — intimate and not intimidating. Yet as she walked in, Erin realised she was more nervous that she'd ever been walking into Dove's with Spencer.

Brad was waiting, looking handsome in cream chinos and a navy shirt. He stood up and pulled back her chair.

'You look lovely,' he murmured close to her ear as she was sitting down.

Erin felt herself blush very red — something that hadn't happened to her for years.

Brad sat down and studied her across the table.

'You look different nearly every time I see you.'

She thought back to what she'd been wearing each time. That first evening at the cottage, when she'd opened the door looking a crumpled mess in those awful trackie bottoms. Then her business suits up at the hotel. This morning she'd turned up in practical jeans and

T-shirt to carry boxes and bags. Tonight, she'd taken a lot of trouble, wanting to impress him.

'Which is the real you?' Brad asked.

Erin still wasn't sure of the answer, or if there was a single answer.

Rosie bustled up to take their order, which meant quickly reading the chalked-up menu board. Both chose the light-sounding crab salad to start.

'How about the chicken for a main course?' Brad suggested.

Erin shook her head rather quickly and told him about her new hens.

He smiled.

'Definitely not the chicken, then.' They agreed on goat's cheese tartlets instead, and Rosie disappeared to the kitchen to give the order to her husband-cum-chef, Oliver.

'You're amassing quite a collection of pets!'

She'd already told him about the cockerel she'd inherited, and the cat who'd been followed closely by her kittens.

'Daph took one of them, Tyson, a few

days ago. My sister's got her name on the other boy.'

'So what did the chickens think of the cats? Or should that be the other way round?'

'The chickens clucked up a bit when the cats turned up to have a look, but they soon settled down again. Feather just sat there, calmly watching. But Mouse, the smallest kitten, came out, and it was so funny!' She gave a broad smile. 'She pretended to stalk them, and Napoleon strutted up and did a funny, Kung-Fu type kick. He was too far away to do any damage, but Mouse turned tail and fled indoors!'

'They all know where they stand, then! When it comes to sharing a space, I sometimes think animals organise themselves far more easily than people.'

'Definitely a lot more straight-forward,' Erin agreed, 'but I guess they don't worry about hurting each other's feelings the way humans do. I'm just glad my little collection seems to have sorted it all out between themselves. Of course,' she added, frowning slightly, 'Mouse will be going once I find her a good home.'

'Sounds like she already has one.'

He had brought a bottle of wine, because Rosie hadn't yet got an alcohol licence for the premises.

'I hope you like white. It's Pinot Grigio, I think.' He turned the label nearer to the candlelight to read.

It was rather dim in the café — or bistro, as it was tonight — but that was all part of the evening's charm.

After pouring them both a glass, Brad raised his to hers.

'To new friendships. And thank you for helping me this morning.'

'That's what friends are for,' she replied, feeling far happier than was necessary for a simple thank you.

Erin found herself relating the circumstances behind her move from Manchester to Norfolk.

'And Spencer, the boyfriend you left behind?'

'Is exactly that,' she replied. 'I went

93

to work for his company straight from school as a trainee, so I'd known him a long time. I've realised it would never have worked out. I never loved him. I know that now.'

Brad nodded slowly. He was a good listener. This new sense of closeness gave her the confidence to ask about his past.

'There was a girl,' he confided softly.

Erin felt a totally unjustified pang of jealousy.

'A long time ago now. I thought she was the one, but as you say, distance brings a different perspective.'

She saw the beginnings of that closed-in, disappointed look descending on his face, and felt determined to keep it at bay. But she'd read him wrongly; he'd chosen not to clam up after all.

'There was an accident, quite a bad one. It was winter, on a patch of black ice. My car, but Jenna had begged to drive it. It just skidded away from us on a bend and ended up upside-down in a ditch.'

Her heart juddered.

'She was killed?'

'No, thank goodness. Jenna walked away with barely a scratch.'

But he hadn't, had he? The slight limp.

'My legs were trapped for several hours until the emergency services were able to cut me free. They were both badly broken in several places. I was in hospital for weeks, and then had months of physiotherapy.'

His expression told Erin how much mental anguish the memories still caused him.

'I had to change my whole way of life. Before that, I was a . . . ' he looked down at his cup ' . . . I was quite sporty before. It was after the accident that I began to study accountancy. Which brings us up to date.'

Not quite. Erin had to ask.

'And your girlfriend?'

'Ah. She decided, as I was no longer the same person, I wasn't right for her after all.'

He made it sound straightforward and matter of course, but she imagined it was still neither of these things for Brad. She'd begun to realise he was a sensitive person, with feelings that ran deep. There was no need to ask if there'd been anyone else since. It was clear he was still nursing a broken heart over the girl who'd changed her mind.

Rosie bustled up with the desserts they'd chosen.

'Strawberry pavlova,' she announced proudly, placing two large plates on the table. 'Oops, forgot the cream. Won't be a sec!' She whizzed away again.

'It's covered in whipped cream already,' Erin whispered to Brad. 'I can feel my waistline grow just looking at it!'

'Never mind your waist, what about my arteries?'

They picked up their spoons and plunged in.

'Hmm, just too gorgeous to resist!' she mumbled.

'Definitely!' he mumbled back, his eyes sparkling.

'My treat,' Brad insisted after coffee had been drunk.

Rosie had discreetly left the bill. But had then spoiled the effect by announcing loudly that she'd given them a resident's discount.

Erin protested about Brad paying, but he was adamant.

'Call me old-fashioned if you like.'

'You're old-fashioned. But I like it. And I'll pay next time.'

Before she had time to kick herself for assuming there would be a next time, Brad replied, 'You're on!'

He was disappointed not to be able to walk her home, and so was Erin. She hadn't thought that far ahead before bringing her car into the village.

'I've just realised,' she said, pausing while ferreting in her bag for the car keys, 'I've had a glass of wine.'

'Leave Mickey here, then, and collect him tomorrow.'

So Brad ended up walking her home after all. He took her arm as they strolled down the street. It was a beautiful June night without the slightest trace of a breeze.

'I still can't get over how bright the stars are in the country,' she said, slowing to lean back and gaze up. 'I must get a book from the library. I'd love to know what all the constellations are.'

'I've got a guide in amongst my books. I'll dig it out it for you.' He pointed up, 'That's The Plough, isn't it? It always looks like a wheelbarrow to me!'

She chuckled.

'And isn't that one Orion?' she said, pointing at another. 'They're all fascinating when you really look at them.' She was turning around, still gazing up, feeling very small and insignificant, and then she became a bit giddy.

'All right?' His hands reached out to steady her.

She nodded, feeling a bit breathless.

'When you think about the universe, it is a bit overwhelming, isn't it?'

She nodded again. What was even more overwhelming was the gentle touch of his hands on her arms.

'I'd hate to live in a city again,' Brad said as they resumed walking.

Erin wondered if she might still have to, but she put such thoughts to the back of her mind.

They'd arrived at the gate to Owl Cottage.

'There you are, home safe and sound. It's been a lovely evening, Erin, thank you. Sweet dreams,' he said, and brushing her cheek with his lips, he turned and left.

He was an old-fashioned gentleman, she thought, closing the door behind her. And she did like that, but she was also slightly disappointed that they hadn't shared a proper kiss. But then again, she felt she was getting to know Brad, and rushing headlong into anything just wasn't his style. Once committed, a relationship with Brad would run deep and true and everlasting.

Was that where his heart would always rest, she wondered with a sigh as she made an absent-minded fuss of the cats. With his first love?

July Visit

Waking up to the sound of a car pulling up outside, Erin fell out of bed and rushed to look out of the bedroom window. It was Elaine, Graham and her nephews, who were already tumbling out of the back seat.

'Auntie Rin, Auntie Rin!' They belted up the path towards the front door and stopped, amazed, when Erin called to them from the upstairs window.

'Are you in the roof?' William gaped.

'You live in a gingerbread house!' James said.

'Sorry we're so early,' Elaine said when she'd clambered from the car. 'The boys were all for starting out before they went to bed!'

'So we compromised, and set out before we'd gone to bed!' Her brother-in-law grinned across the car seats.

Erin, who'd rushed downstairs still

wearing her pyjamas, was astonished at how big her sister had got in the three months since she'd seen her.

'Have you got twins in there?' she asked, giving her a hug and then turning to her brother-in-law.

'We'd better not have!' Graham grinned, blinking in the sun. 'Phew, so this is where the summer went.' He stretched his long frame and sighed luxuriantly. 'Oh, it's good to get out of the car. Well, this all looks very charming, Erin.'

'Be prepared to fold yourself up again,' Elaine told him, 'because you haven't seen inside yet.'

'We have,' the boys chorused, running out of the front door, 'and look what we found!' William had claimed his long-awaited kitten and was holding him in his arms already. James was cradling Mouse.

Elaine's eyes widened silently at Erin. She could guess what her sister was thinking. Would the boys want one each?

'We'll cross that bridge when the

time comes,' Graham said wisely.

'You mean I will!' Elaine protested.

Erin smiled. She loved her sister and brother-in-law's double act.

After nipping back upstairs to throw on some shorts and a strappy top, Erin gave them all a quick tour of the cottage, followed by the garden, which took a lot longer. The boys were fascinated by the chickens in their run.

'More animals?' Elaine gasped. 'I dread to think what you'll have next time I come!'

'Not animals, Mummy!' James scolded. 'Chickens are birds.'

'I stand corrected.'

'You're going to find this hard to leave behind,' Graham said, giving her a concerned look.

'I'm trying not to think about it,' Erin replied, leading everyone inside again. The heat was already intense and there wasn't a cloud in the sky. She put the kettle on, made squash for the boys and set about rustling up scrambled eggs for everyone.

After breakfast, the boys were still full of bounce, but Elaine was flagging a bit after such an early start. Graham decided it was time they got settled into their hotel, the idea being to occupy the boys while Elaine put her feet up for half an hour.

Erin had arranged for them to stay at Greensides. Jim Standing had offered a discounted rate on a family room, a generous gesture on his part as trade had picked up considerably and there were very few spare rooms available.

'Now, this I'm really looking forward to,' Elaine said gleefully while Graham rounded up the boys and tried separating them from the kittens. 'I can't wait to meet your Brad.'

'Well, you'll have to, until this evening. And he's not my Brad,' Erin protested. They'd had a few more dates and there was a distinct growing warmth between them, but their relationship was still at the friendship stage.

'You think he's still haunted by the ghost of the girlfriend past?'

Erin pulled a face and shook her head at the same time, which neatly summed up her confusion.

'I'm sure you'll be able to make him forget all about her, once and for all!' Elaine prophesied.

It would have been nice to think so, but Erin wasn't convinced. Despite opening up considerably over the last few weeks, Brad still kept a lot bottled up. She would dearly love to know whether it was because he didn't want to burden her with his past disappointments, or because he didn't yet trust her enough.

But for whatever reason he held a part of himself in reserve, Erin only hoped it was something that time would ultimately resolve, but nearly five months of her leap year had passed already.

More immediately, this was the start of Erin's week as church key-holder. With arrangements in place to meet up with them later, Erin waved her family off to the hotel while she headed down to the village on foot to unlock All Saints' for the day.

An early evening table had been booked at Greensides, to cover the boys' tea and the adults' dinner in one sitting. Brad, after a lot of convincing that he wouldn't be intruding or in the way, had agreed to join them. The early timing worked well for him, too, as he planned on catching the last train of the day from Norwich down to Essex, to stay overnight and Sunday with his sister.

Erin picked him up as arranged at a quarter to six that evening on her way through the village. That gave her the opportunity to lock up All Saints' for the night, after a quick check round that no late sightseer was still inside. Anne Grange had told her that she'd once nearly locked someone in by mistake!

'Look!' Brad had come inside with Erin. He was pointing to the day's entries in the visitors' book.

Someone had written how much they

appreciated finding the church open.

Really made my day.

'There, you did that!' Brad smiled as they got back into her car.

Erin felt her face go pink, and couldn't deny a sense of pride at having played her part in improving someone's visit to Brundenham. It went hand-in-hand with the work she'd done with the parish council, getting the village's name associated with other venues rich in cultural and heritage links.

'I'd have suggested we all eat at Rosie's Bistro,' she told Brad, 'but there wouldn't have been enough space with the four of us and the boys. We'd have had to take over the whole place!'

'Bistro bookings are up again, so Rosie tells me. Word's getting around that she's open on weekend evenings.'

'Autumn will be the test,' Erin mused, 'when the local people start hunkering down indoors.'

She was quite looking forward to those sorts of evening herself. But when they came it would also mean the year was turning . . . and turning far too fast for her liking.

She wasn't aware she'd given a sigh until Brad spoke.

'It's not that bad, is it?'

'What?'

'The prospect of your family meeting me!'

'Silly!' She smiled at him.

'I'm looking forward to meeting them, after all you've told me about them.'

'There they all are,' Erin said as she pulled into Greensides' car-park, spotting her family enjoying the lawns at the front of the hotel.

Elaine was first to spot their arrival, and came over while Graham was refereeing a small squabble that had broken out between the boys.

'I was hoping they'd be tired, after such an early start,' Elaine said. 'But no such luck. I'm more whacked than they are!'

'Overtired,' Brad suggested, giving her a smile.

Elaine nodded, and put out her hand.

'It's lovely to meet you at last, Brad. Erin never stops talking about you.'

Erin gasped, and made furious eye signals.

'Only because you never let me!'

'Now, now, girls!' Graham shook his head with mock severity as he came over and shook Brad's hand. 'Very pleased to meet you. Boys, come here, please. Now, remember what we do?'

William and Jamie were duly introduced. Erin couldn't help smiling as they solemnly shook hands just as their dad had shown them.

'He's nice,' Elaine whispered. 'And even better-looking than I remembered!'

Erin gave her a sceptical look. Elaine had only got the barest glimpse of Brad in the café.

Erin hadn't realised how tense she'd been about the meeting until the relief set in. Everyone was getting on just fine.

'I don't know why you don't think

he's yours.' Elaine leaned into Erin during dinner. Brad was busy talking with Graham. 'You should see the way he looks at you.'

'Can you sense that air of sadness about him, Elaine, or is it just me?'

'A bit, perhaps, but it disappears when he looks at you, that's for sure. I tell you, Erin, I'm certain he's smitten.'

Erin's heart strummed at the idea.

'I just wish he'd say something, or give some sort of hint.' Or kiss her. That would do it.

'What are you two whispering about?' Graham suddenly demanded.

'Nothing!' they chorused indignantly, sharing a smile.

'You should have let me run you to the station,' Erin said once they were in the car and on the way back to the Rosy Leaf. Brad had ordered a taxi to collect him from there to take him to Norwich station. 'We'd have had plenty of time.'

By the time they'd eaten, the boys had finally shown signs of slowing down, and Elaine was keen to turn in early, so Erin and Brad had left while it was still relatively early.

'I know, Erin, and thanks for the offer, but I don't want you to have to keep running me about.'

It was hardly that often. If they went anywhere outside of the village, Erin drove them, but it was always a joint decision to go any further afield.

'You know I don't mind,' she told him, feeling disappointed. She'd have enjoyed the chance to spend a bit longer together on the drive to Norwich.

So much for Elaine's certainty that Brad was smitten. She'd yet to see any great sign of it.

'You've got a great family,' Brad reflected. 'And a lovely relationship with your sister.'

'I'm pleased you like them, and yes, Elaine and I are lucky. We've always got on well together.' She knew it wasn't always the case with sisters, especially ones so close in age. 'Do you get on well with your sister?'

'Not bad,' Brad said in a drawn-out,

thoughtful way. 'But we've never been really close. Kelly was twelve when I was born. When I was old enough to want to tag along she was a teenager, and didn't want to be stuck with a kid brother hanging on and cramping her style!'

'What about your parents, Brad?'

'Dad walked out not long after I was born. I don't think it was entirely because of me!' He gave a small chuckle that wasn't entirely convincing.

'Mum eventually remarried, but only quite recently. Her new husband has a holiday place in Spain, and now they've both retired they've moved there permanently. I've been out to see them a couple of times, and she's happy, finally happy, at last. It's good to see.'

Erin's driving was getting slower and slower. She didn't want to arrive in the village and stop Brad's flow. It was rare that he opened up like this.

'So what about your dad?' Erin asked softly. 'Do you ever see him?'

He shook his head.

'He never kept in touch.'

'Oh, Brad.' She couldn't help reaching out and squeezing his hand. Then she was dismayed when he flinched before pulling it away.

'What you've never had you never miss.' He added lightly, 'Or isn't that what they say?'

'I'm not sure it's true,' she murmured. She still missed her own mum and dad, and it often hurt to think about them not being around anymore. But, then, that was a paltry price to pay for having such lovely, loving parents.

Surely Brad's stance was more about him putting up a wall again to shield behind.

He shrugged.

'It hit Kelly much harder than me. I can't remember our dad at all, but obviously she did. She went off the rails for a while, but settled down again, thank goodness. And she's been a brick over looking after Walt for me.'

In the main street now, Erin let the car roll to a halt outside the Rosy Leaf.

''Walt? Oh, your dog. Short for Walter?'

'Short for Walthamstow.' He grinned. 'That's where I found him, wandering around the outside of the greyhound track. No-one ever came forward to claim him, so we've stuck together ever since.'

Erin could hear the fondness in his voice.

With a quick peck on the cheek and a promise to ring her when he got back, Brad got out and Erin continued on to Owl Cottage, never getting higher than third gear. For once, it wasn't Metal Mickey's fault. She had a lot to think about.

Brad's reaction had been illuminating, but only up to a point. He clearly didn't like sympathy. Did that stem back to his childhood, or from the more recent car accident? Erin wished she knew more about his ex-girlfriend, Jenna. Had she been sympathetic at first about his injuries? Had she supported him through his slow recovery?

According to Brad she'd left him as he wasn't right for her anymore. Because he was no longer the same person. That meant, if she'd behaved sympathetic and supportive to Brad's face, then had turned around and left him, no wonder he was wary of sympathy. Why risk the pain again with someone new?

A small voice in Erin's brain said that you couldn't choose who you fell in love with. It either happened or it didn't. If she fell in love with Brad, for example, there wouldn't be much she could do about it, except to try to pretend it wasn't happening, of course.

Supposition about Brad and flights of imagination on her behalf. It wasn't a sensible combination, especially when you were tired. She was yawning as she let herself into the cottage and the cats came to greet her. It had been an earlier start than usual for her, too. A busy day, and an even busier one ahead tomorrow. After a quick check to make sure Napoleon and his harem were secure inside their run, she decided on an early night for herself.

For Sunday, Erin had devised a local sightseeing itinerary for her family which concluded back at the village close on teatime. They had had an interesting exploration of All Saints' church, the life-sized marble monument of a mediaeval soldier in full battle-dress proving a particularly popular attraction.

It was just about time for Erin to lock up for the day. The boys were thrilled when she asked them to do it. They were fascinated by the size, weight and feel of the giant iron key, and considered it a great honour to be allowed to perform what their dad called the 'Closing Ceremony'. He rolled up his copy of the guide pamphlet and blew a 'ta-ta-ta-tata-taaaa' as they solemnly turned the key.

'I'm going to tell Miss Watson I locked up the church!' William boasted.

'You can't,' Jamie argued. 'Because she's not your teacher anymore. She's my teacher now, isn't she, Mum?'

'Not until September,' Elaine arbitrated. 'So at the moment she belongs to both of you. September!' she enthused softly to Erin, while rubbing the small of her back and smiling with fondness at her sons. 'I can't decide whether it's hurtling towards us far too quickly, or can't come soon enough!'

Erin sympathised, but knew which one she'd plump for.

'Elaine, we really ought to be making tracks,' Graham announced, sounding less than enthusiastic.

The boys groaned.

'But you're taking back a kitten,' Erin reminded them, and they cheered up again.

Elaine said she fancied a cup of tea before starting out. Unfortunately, Rosy Leaf was closed on Sundays, so Erin was just about to suggest going back to Owl Cottage when they bumped into Daph. She'd come to the churchyard to lay flowers on her parents' grave.

'You must all come back to mine,' she insisted. 'Pete and I haven't seen you for days, Erin. And he'd love to meet the rest of your lovely family,' she added, smiling all round.

Seated around Daph's generous table in the bungalow's spacious kitchen, Elaine started quizzing her and Pete about Brad.

'We've not met him yet,' Daph told her, 'but I've noticed the way Erin looks when she talks about him.'

Erin gave a huff.

'The way you all go on, anyone would think I'm talking about him all the while!'

Daph and Elaine shared a look, before chorusing, 'You are!'

It had been a lovely weekend, Erin reflected as they parted. The boys were delighted with their new kitten, upon whom had now been bestowed the grand name of King Arthur. Apparently the ancient key to the church had reminded the boys of castles, and from there it had been a short association to knights, round tables and the royal monarch himself.

'Well, we're not taking Guinevere to go with him.' Graham put Mouse back firmly in Erin's arms.

'No, just think how much Feather would miss her if we took her as well,' Elaine said, which convinced them.

'Phew!' she breathed out of the corner of her mouth. 'That was a close one!'

August Revelations

Erin was meant to be working. She'd set her laptop up on the kitchen worktop, but was beginning to think it had been a mistake to put it there. The view from the window was distracting. Today, the cornfield out the back was being harvested. The waist-high crop was being quickly transformed into huge circular bales. It was totally absorbing and fascinating watching the huge combine-harvester go back and forth, reminding her of a shuttle on a loom, weaving a new pattern on the landscape.

She lifted the lid on her laptop and waited for it to hum into life. As well as trying to formulate some ideas for a prospective client, she also had to get in touch with Brad. He'd called her up rather late last night.

'Another favour to ask, Erin. This is a

bit more of a serious commitment, though.'

For a split second, her stupid heart had fluttered.

'Kelly, my sister, is moving from Essex. Her partner's been transferred to a branch on the south coast, so they're relocating down there at the end of the month.'

'Oh,' she began, wondering where this was leading. Then she suddenly had a thought. 'What about Walt?'

'They can't take him. Their new place is an apartment.'

'So you wondered if I could take him?'

A greyhound? With cats and chickens? It was hardly a recipe for domestic harmony.

But on the other hand, she felt sorry for poor Walt, the stray that no-one had claimed. Erin knew, from how he talked about Walt, just how much this dog meant to him.

'Would it work, do you think, Erin? It would only be for a month or two. I'm determined to find somewhere more suitable to live as soon as anything comes up.'

That could mean him leaving the village, even the area. Her stomach plummeted.

'I don't see why we couldn't give it a try . . . '

'Sleep on it, Erin. I'd rather you were really sure.'

'If it'll make you happy, I'll call you back tomorrow.'

No new problem or difficulty had come to her overnight. In fact, she was looking forward to it now — she'd wanted a dog, hadn't she? Hopefully she and Walt would take to each other. Also, hopefully, her other inmates would budge up and get used to the new arrangement, too!

* * *

With the hot sun beating down, Erin was taking a slow walk back from the village when she saw Pete Carr's van heading towards her. He slowed down. The window already dropped down, he leaned out.

'Hey, have you got any plans for this evening?'

'Nothing much. The veg patch needs watering.' There was always something to do in the garden.

She had no definite plans to see Brad. Some evenings he wandered up to Owl Cottage to see her. After lending her a hand with anything she was doing, they'd sit outside as the dusk fell, sharing a bottle of wine and chatting. They'd watch Napoleon and the hens take themselves off to roost, which was quite a performance sometimes, and after that they'd watch the stars come out.

'The watering shouldn't take you too long,' Pete said now. 'And the hedges will still be there tomorrow. So do you fancy coming to the match with me and Daph?'

'Match?'

Pete rolled his eyes.

'Down th' Carrer Rood, of course!'

'Ah, football!' Erin had learned that 'Carrer Rood' was the Norfolk-accented version of Carrow Road, the home of Norwich City Football Club.

'It's only August, it can't have started up again already.'

'Pre-season friendly,' Pete said enjoyably. 'Give us a chance to see what our new summer signings are capable of. Only, we've a couple of spare tickets, if you're interested. Why not ask that young man of yours along? Daph was saying the other day that we've still not met him.'

Erin still couldn't assume that Brad was 'hers', but going to a football match would be a novel experience. She'd no idea if Brad was a football follower or not. Still, there was only one way to find out.

'Sounds great, Pete, thanks. Count me in. I'll see if Brad's free. What time will you be leaving?'

'We'll pick you up about six. That'll give us time to get parked and into the ground.'

* * *

'Hi, Erin.'

She was getting used to her heart doing a little juggling act whenever she heard Brad's voice, even if it was only down the phone.

'Just a quick call, Brad, because I know you're still at work. Only, I've just bumped into Pete Carr. He and Daph have offered to take us out tonight to the football. The Norwich City match. How about it?'

The silence from the other end of the phone was so absolute that for a second she thought they'd been cut off.

'Are you still there?'

'Yes, I'm here.' His tone was clipped and sharp. 'But, no thanks.'

And then the phone did go dead. Brad had put down the phone. Just like that. Perhaps someone had come into the room, or there had been a call coming through on the office landline? He'd probably ring back in a moment or two.

She tapped a few keys on her laptop as she waited, but couldn't concentrate on the work. She put the kettle on to boil, keeping the phone within earshot. The minutes ticked away . . .

Brad wasn't going to call back. He'd said no. Was it the fact she'd asked him out, or that they'd be going with Pete and Daph? But he'd never met them. Was it football he wasn't keen on, then? But why such a blunt refusal?

Bewildered, she called the Carrs. Daph answered.

'Hello, lovey. I hope you're still coming tonight.'

'If you're sure,' she said, injecting brightness into her voice. 'Unfortunately Brad can't make it.'

'That's a shame.'

'I thought I'd better let you know, in case there's someone else for the other ticket, or even another couple.'

But Daph was adamant that Erin should still go, and they picked her up as arranged.

'Shame about Brad not being able to

make it.' Pete turned round to Erin once she was in the back seat.

Erin flushed, feeling a bit guilty. She didn't want to explain Brad's reaction over the phone. How could she, when she didn't understand it herself? And it was definitely no reason to spoil Daph and Pete's evening.

'Never mind, I'm sure you'll still enjoy yourself,' Daph said as they left the village at the roundabout and joined the road into Norwich. 'And when you next see him you can tell him what he's missed.'

'Plenty of yellow and green goals, I hope!' Pete waved his scarf.

Nearly everyone had a scarf, and several supporters were wearing matching bobble hats despite the intense and humid heat of the evening. It felt like a holiday carnival atmosphere to Erin, as she, Pete and Daph joined the chattering, bustling fans making their way hurriedly through the streets.

Inside, the ground was a real sun trap, too. Erin found she didn't need the light jacket she'd worn, and laid it across her knees. Shielding her eyes to see certain parts of the pitch, she wondered how the players coped during the game, and had a sudden bizarre image of them running around wearing sunglasses.

'Glad you seem to be enjoying yourself now you're here,' Daph said, catching her smile.

'No, it's great, and I'm so glad you and Pete asked me along. It's a real education.'

'I can't believe you've never been to a football match,' Daph said when they'd reached their seats. 'And you a Manchester girl, too.'

'It's unforgivable really!' Erin shouted to be heard over the roaring pop music. 'And I used to live not far from Maine Road into the bargain.' She supposed she still did, as the flat was still technically rented in her name. Goodness, she hadn't given a thought to her previous place in weeks. It felt like another life now.

'You haven't missed much by not watching them or United.' Pete winked. 'We play the real game over here! Here we go, the Canaries are coming out now . . . Come on, you yellers!'

The chanting roared into life along with a huge cheer as the yellow-and-green-kitted team trotted on to the pitch. After the preliminaries of warming up, hand-shaking, and tossing the coin, accompanied by constant announcements over the tannoy, finally the game kicked off.

And it was exciting in parts, completely different in real life from the snatches she'd caught on television. It was the atmosphere that made it, as the crowd oohed and aahed with every kick, pass and dribble. But there were also periods where the ball just passed endlessly back and forth, and Erin found her mind meandering in a similar fashion.

She just couldn't forget Brad's curt response over the phone. That cold, sharp, emphatic no. No apology, no explanation. It was so unlike him. He was always so polite, considerate. Reserved, yes, but never rude. But then, she'd not known him all that long, really, had she?

Erin counted back the months. The first time she'd seen him had been her moving in day. And the second time, when they'd passed in the café, had been a month later. So it was her visit to the hotel in May before she'd really started to get to know him. Just over three months ago. Was it possible to fall in love that quickly?

And whoever said anything about being in love with him? Erin caught herself up sharply. She suspected she might be, though. And she was beginning to think he had developed feelings for her, too, which had made his reaction on the phone so inexplicable. In fact, his attitude almost made her feel angry . . .

'Yep, I know how you feel! Nil-nil after forty-five, and all those wasted chances!' It was Pete, gently elbowing her in the ribs, which told her she must have been grimacing. She hadn't even realised, nor that the first half of the game was over. The players were jogging off the pitch, and many of the supporters were bustling down the aisles.

'A lot can happen in the next forty-five minutes,' Daph remarked, and Pete gave her a look that said there was nothing like stating the obvious.

Pete stood and stretched his bones.

'Oh, that's better. Come on, girls, let's get some food before it all goes.'

'Steak and kidney pie and a mug of tea,' Daph explained. 'All part of the experience.'

Even before the second half started, Erin decided she was going to concentrate more on the game and less on Brad Cavill. In the event, the second half was a lot more thrilling, with real end-to-end play. Several Norwich players had more chances, which were either missed or saved. Huge agonising wails went up each time. Finally the Canaries' star striker headed the ball from inside the penalty area, and it went soaring into the top right corner of the net.

The crowd shot to their feet as one, Erin included, and everyone went wild. The noise was deafening. The scoring player ran over to the Canary fans behind the goal, his team members in congratulatory pursuit, and performed a dance that looked comical to Erin's eyes. But the crowd were thrilled and, clearly familiar with it, egged him on as if each of them had had a share in scoring the goal.

And Erin suddenly saw the attraction of the game, for its team players and supporters. The anticipation, the anguish, the successes and failures. The feeling of being a part of something. It was powerful, emotional stuff.

'I had a really good time,' she told Pete and Daph on the drive back to Brundenham. 'Thanks so much for asking me.'

'Pity it was just the one goal,' Pete said, who had nevertheless still not stopped smiling since the opposition goalkeeper had dispiritedly picked the ball out of the back of the away net. 'But it was a good, promising performance. Especially from the new signings. That's the main thing. Augurs very well for when the new season kicks off proper. Not long to wait now, either.'

Someone else wishing the year away, Erin thought, watching Pete rubbing his hands together delightedly. The excitement shone from his sparkling eyes, and Daph's, too. They were a close couple, Erin thought, and reminded her of Elaine and Graham in many ways. She felt a sudden pang of loneliness.

'Can I carry on riding with you into the village?' she asked impulsively as Daph changed down a gear approaching Erin's lane. 'I might just see if Brad's around.' She caught Daph and Pete exchanging a look.

'What?'

'I said to Pete earlier that I thought you two might have had a tiff.'

Erin felt herself going pink, but had no idea how to respond. Glancing out of the side window, she caught sight of a familiar figure walking along the narrow pavement.

Brad.

'There he is!' she exclaimed.

Daph hit the brakes, then put the car into reverse. The gearbox complained loudly.

'It's OK, I can get out here,' Erin protested.

'He's heading your way.' Pete said, turning around to see. 'I bet he was going round to yours to wait for you to come home.'

'To make up,' Daph said with a smile.

Brad had noticed the car reversing and turned back to meet it. Daph stopped for a second time, and Erin prepared to get out.

'So that's your Brad?' Pete's brow furrowed thoughtfully. 'What's his second name?'

'Cavill. Why?'

Daph was peering out with interest, too.

Pete struck his forehead with his palm.

'Brad Cavill! Got him now. Thought I recognised his face. He used to play professionally, didn't he?'

'Until he had that accident,' Daph added.

In one fell swoop, Erin understood Brad's reaction to the football match invitation. Or thought she did. And if she was right, she knew Brad well enough now to realise that he wouldn't want to discuss his feelings in front of Daph and Pete. And they were bound to want to talk about the match they'd just watched.

Before they could suggest her and Brad coming back to theirs, Erin put a hand on each of their shoulders.

'We have had a bit of a row. Would you mind if I spared the introductions this time and just whisked him away?'

'Of course. We understand, lovey.' Daph patted her hand.

Pete nodded.

'Never let it be said that the Carrs stand in the way of true love!'

Daph looked at him fondly and tutted.

With a rapid but heartfelt word of thanks, Erin scrambled out of the back seat. Without looking at Brad, she went and stood by his side, waving as the car pulled away.

'Daph and Pete?'

'Hmm.'

'Did you have a good time at the game?' She murmured again.

His hand squeezed her free one, and finally she turned to face him.

'Sorry, Erin,' he said simply.

The light was fading, but still strong enough to search his eyes. They were darker tonight. So much pain there, it made her own heart ache.

She reached out and touched his face.

'Come on. Let's go back to Owl Cottage. We can talk better there.'

It was where he'd been heading, apparently, to wait for her to get back. To explain about why he'd been like he had on the phone.

'The more I thought about it, the more I wanted to kick myself,' he said ruefully, when they'd settled themselves on the sofa.

Erin had made mugs of coffees, which were lying cooling and untouched on the coffee table. Mouse was doing her best to attract attention, looking incredibly cute as she rolled on the floor by their feet, wrestling with a catnip toy. Feather sat watching them from the other chair, blinking her beautiful eyes from time to time.

'How could you have any idea that I'd once been a professional footballer?'

'I've never followed the game,' she admitted.

'Even if you had, there was no reason why you'd have heard of me anyway. My team was in a very minor league.'

Erin was having trouble relocating the Brad she'd come to know into the same scenario as the game she'd just watched. The football players that hit the headlines, and the ones she'd watched on the pitch tonight, were a mixture, in varying degrees, of aggression and melo-dramatics. Two characteristics she'd never witnessed in Brad or would ever dream of associating him with.

'It's a different world in the lower league,' he said, as if reading her mind. 'No superstar egos or histrionics down there. It's just a case of getting on with it. I'd been playing for the same team down in Essex for seven years, ever since I left school.'

'Is it something you always wanted to do?'

Brad shook his head firmly.

'That was the odd thing. I played in the school team, no better and no worse than any of the others, I thought. But this local club had a talent scout who they'd send round to all the schools. Clearly he saw some potential, and recommended me to the club, who signed me up when I was seventeen. I still wasn't convinced I was any good. I kept thinking they'd realise I was dud eventually. But even if I ended up out on my ear at the end of the first season, it seemed too good an opportunity to let slip.'

Erin nodded. She could imagine most sixteen- or seventeen-year-olds would jump at the chance of playing football for a living.

'I quite enjoyed playing, but I'd never been football-mad or anything, like some of my mates. They lived and breathed the game. To be honest, though, it saved me the trouble of going out and finding myself a proper job.'

'So what happened then?'

'I played for that club for about seven years. We'd go up a league one season, down the next. The club was small, but had a loyal fan base, and it was solvent, which you couldn't say for every outfit in those days. Or now,' he added.

'So which position did you play?'

'I was one of the strikers. For six years I scored just an average amount of goals each season, but then suddenly everything went right. It didn't feel as if I was playing any differently, but I just couldn't put a foot wrong. Every time I got a chance with the ball, it ended up in the back of the net. My goal tally that seventh season with them broke all records of any league.'

There was no trace of a boast in his voice, Erin noted. She sensed he'd rehearsed what he was going to tell her, not for any deceptive purposes, but to protect himself. The hurt had gone deep.

'The local press covered our progress that season, and they went typically over the top. Football's a small world, and a couple of scouts from London clubs came to watch me play. The upshot was, at twenty-four, I'd become an overnight guaranteed goal-scoring machine. Suddenly I was hot property. Articles in the national press. Kids wanting autographs. Girls waiting outside the ground at the end of every match.'

'One in particular?' Erin's voice was almost a whisper. She didn't even want to ask, but couldn't stop herself.

'Jenna. Yes.' Brad spoke flatly, his eyes on Mouse. 'That's how we met.'

'And then the accident happened?' Erin prompted softly.

'Just as I was on the point of signing for West Ham. To be honest, I couldn't believe it was happening to me. I expected to be with my Essex club until they chucked me out. Both clubs were sympathetic, but I was no good to either after the damage to my legs.'

The end of his career and his relationship with Jenna. What a blow that must have been.

Brad was looking at her, his expression tortured and regretful.

'The crazy thing was, I never knew how much my football meant to me until I could no longer play. I don't mean the glamour or the huge pay packet, although the money would have been great, of course. But unless you enjoy the sort of constant attention that goes with it, I think it's a high price to pay for your loss of privacy.'

Erin nodded. From what she knew of Brad, she could understand him feeling that way about it.

'It was my health and fitness that I took for granted, too. But to know that

I'll never play again, full stop . . . It's seven years ago now, but I still can't come to terms with it.'

There must be other things he could do, she mused. Some sort of involvement, on the training side, perhaps. But one look at his face stopped her from speaking.

'I don't think I'll ever get over it.' His voice was so quiet, it was almost impossible to make out the words, yet somehow that made them all the more powerful.

She reached out, and pulled her to him. For a few seconds she held on to him.

'I'm so sorry, Brad.'

'Not sympathy, please, Erin,' he groaned, as he pulled away from her. 'Not from you, of all people.'

She was confused. She'd suspected before that he was uncomfortable with sympathy. But why not from her, specifically?

Then he was reaching out for her again.

'Sorry, that was hurtful. I know there's no side with your sympathy.'

So this was to do with his ex-girlfriend, Jenna. He was comparing Erin to her. Jenna had been sympathetic initially, hadn't she? But she had then gone on to dump Brad, saying that he was no longer the person she'd thought he was.

Erin felt a wave of fury on Brad's behalf. He hadn't changed, but his prospects had. No longer a Premiership footballer in the making, with all the glamour and financial rewards that offered. That was what had driven Jenna away, not his failure to come to terms with the repercussions of the accident.

Surely Brad could see that?

'Jenna never really loved me. It didn't take me long to work that one out. But I was dazzled by her at the start. I just couldn't believe someone as lovely as her would be interested in someone like me.'

Erin shook her head with a small smile.

'You underestimate your attractiveness, you know,' she murmured shyly, and so quietly she didn't think he even heard her. She longed to touch him again, badly wanted to kiss away his hurt.

'She was petite, with long blonde hair.' Brad reached out and touched Erin's hair. She was conscious that it was tousled, knotted and probably gritty from her evening at the match and the walk back to the car through the breezy, dusty streets. She had an image now of Jenna as the typical WAG as seen in the tabloid papers, glossy, glamorous and well-groomed.

'Remember your first evening here, and you answered the door to me? For a split second I thought it was Jenna I was seeing standing there.'

Erin swallowed an incredulous cry. If she remembered correctly, she'd looked a mess then as well, crumpled from sleep and wearing those awful tracksuit bottoms that she'd since thrown away. It would explain the way Brad had taken a startled half step backwards.

OK, so Erin had the long blonde hair

and she was reasonably petite. Perhaps she should feel flattered to be even momentarily compared with the lovely Jenna. Perhaps she might resemble her, superficially at least.

But Erin would never have abandoned the man she loved, particularly when he needed her the most. She looked intently at Brad, desperately hoping he could see that, too.

'I was relieved when I realised it wasn't her,' Brad said, his voice dropping to a whisper. 'I'm so glad, Erin, that you're you.'

His kiss took her by surprise. It was light and sweet — and far too short. Little more than a brushing of the lips really. Before she had time to realise it was happening, let alone respond, it was over. He'd drawn back from her.

But when she looked into his eyes, they were so deep she could almost drown there. She realised with a jolt that the barriers had gone. He was allowing her in close for a brief moment, and an unspoken dialogue was taking place.

He seemed as surprised as she was at what was happening. Could it be because the connection between them was undeniable?

September Warmth

Although the September evenings were starting to pull in, the dawns were still breaking early. Erin loved to rise as soon as she woke and take a cup of tea and sit out the back on fine mornings, even if the air was chilly and she had to hunker down in a fleecy dressing-gown. The sun rose over the woods across the fields, and watching the sky behind them change from gold through pink, pale lemon and finally to blue was a spectacular sight.

The cats would accompany her, and make token stalks and pounces at the hens as they emerged from the shed. But they and Napoleon were wise to the game by now, and rarely took any notice. Napoleon had been a changed bird since the arrival of his wives and he'd actually started to crow occasionally.

Mouse, the smaller third kitten, had grown almost as large as her mum Feather. And she had, as Brad and everyone else had suspected all along, become a permanent resident at Owl Cottage. Mouse was more openly affectionate than her mother, and definitely more playful. She was swiping at the dangling end of Erin's dressing-gown tie now.

'Come on, you,' Erin said, distracting her with a blade of grass. 'I've got to get up and get on.'

It was a Saturday, and strictly she didn't have anything specific to do. Or nothing she felt very enthusiastic about making a start on. Another review of her finances was overdue, plus some more tweaks to the business website, with the aim of attracting more enquiries. She desperately needed more paying clients.

Her work was all but finished at Greensides Hotel. Jim Standing had pronounced himself very satisfied with the resulting increase in bookings and the hotel's enhanced status, image-wise.

He'd passed her name on to several of his colleagues in the trade, and she'd received a few enquiries.

After preparing and submitting several proposals, all the feedback had been positive but none, unfortunately, had resulted in a contract. The financial downturn, of course, was global and national, not just local, but its effects were the same. Not many businesses dared risking money on anything that wasn't considered an absolute essential. Even if, as Erin was quick to point out, projecting the right image was crucial in a financial climate where consumers were ever more selective over where they spent their hard-earned money.

She was still doing work helping to promote the image of Brundenham and the surrounding area. The village was now linked with other nearby tourist spot websites, and she'd managed to get it included on a couple of coach firms' itineraries. The resulting increase in profile and visitor numbers had been satisfying, but the work was on a voluntary basis; which she was happy to do as a contribution to her life there. She enjoyed feeling a part of the community who'd made her so welcome.

However, although she hated to admit it, Spencer may well have been right to cast scepticism on her choice of location to set up on her own. Rural firms tended to be either branches of huge corporations who employed their own in-house image consultants, or else smaller firms who didn't see the need and definitely couldn't afford such services.

With the fine weather holding out, Erin decided to strip the bed and put on a load of washing. Household chores always made her feel virtuous, even if they were sometimes something of a diversionary tactic. That done, she looked at the laptop, then looked at her phone.

She decided to ring Elaine first.

'Hiya,' Elaine chirped. 'I was just thinking about you. What are you up to?'

'Not much. Just wondering what I'm going to do from here on in.'

'Oh, dear. This sounds serious. Let me sit down ... right, I'm down. Whether I'll ever manage to get upright again is something else! Now, what's up? Is it Brad, work, or what?'

'Both. Everything.' Erin suddenly felt guilty. 'But you've got enough on your plate at the moment, Elaine. Are you sure you want to listen to this ... '

'Look, my ankles ache, my back aches, and I'm waddling round like a giant duck! Anything that takes my mind off that is fine with me.'

Erin chuckled.

'You're making me feel better already. It's work, mainly. Not enough of it. I'm beginning to think Spencer was right all along.'

At the other end of the line, Elaine sucked in her breath.

'That man was never right, not for you personally, anyway.'

'No, but he knows his stuff when it come to business.'

'Hmm. What does Brad think?'

Erin shrugged.

'Wouldn't I love to know. Actually,' she rushed on, 'he's always very supportive of what I'm trying to achieve with the business, but he's the first to admit he doesn't have a clue about how it all works. He's always trying to come up with ideas to attract some more clients, though.'

'And is Brad thinking of anything else that you'd love to know about?'

Erin couldn't help smiling. There was never any heading off the subject where Elaine was concerned.

'Us,' she admitted, equally directly. 'He's opened up a lot since we had that conversation about the end of his footballing career.' And that kiss, she added silently to herself. 'We're growing closer, I think, but . . . '

'But he's still the strong, silent type?'

'You're telling me.'

Perhaps he always would be. She liked those aspects of his character. She only wished she knew if he felt about her the way she did about him.

'Perhaps I should just accept that he takes a long time to allow anyone in really close.'

'If I were two hundred miles closer and three stones lighter, I'd run round right now and knock your heads together!'

'You couldn't!' Erin retorted. 'Brad's down in Essex, at his sister's. He's collecting his dog.'

'Oh, yes, it's Walt Day, you told me. Another animal in that tiny cottage. How will you fit them all in? You're turning into that woman with all the children who lived in the shoe.'

'You can talk, Mrs Mother Earth.'

'Yeah, well, half of my predicament is Graham's fault. And this house is more of a shoebox than a shoe.'

'The extension not coming on as fast as you'd like?'

'You can say that again.' Elaine sighed. 'Only please don't. Graham's mad enough with the builder as it is.'

'See, I said you had enough on your

plate without hearing my woes.'

'But yours are so much more fascinating than my ordinary old domestic ones,' Elaine said.

When Erin put the phone down, she was feeling brighter, as she always did whenever she spoke to her sister. Though she wasn't sure if trailing back to Manchester next March, broke and jobless, would be all that fascinating. In fact, her heart was sinking at the prospect. And the idea of leaving Brundenham and parting from Brad made it almost crack in two. She really needed to toughen up, make plans. So at least if the worse came to the worst, she might stand a chance of dealing with it.

★ ★ ★

Erin couldn't have been more surprised when Brad got off the train and at the other end of the lead he held was not a greyhound, but a brown and white collie-type dog. What had happened to Walt?

'Hello there, boy!' Erin bent down to make a fuss of the dog anyway.

He was cautious and reserved to begin with, but after giving her a thorough sniff, she seemed to pass muster, and his long tongue came out and swept over her face.

'Walt!' Brad jangled the lead. 'You're supposed to be on your best behaviour and making a good impression. Sorry about that, Erin.'

But Erin was laughing as she wiped her face.

'He's lovely. I expected him to be a greyhound. Because of the Walthamstow connection,' she explained.

'Oh, right. No, he was just wandering round outside the stadium.'

'Perhaps the sound of the other dogs drew him there.'

'Or perhaps he thinks he's long-legged, elegant and sleek, instead of being a lovable lump,' Brad suggested.

Erin, feeling light-hearted, hooked her arm through Brad's as the three of them made their way from Thorpe station and back to where she'd parked her car.

It was the same place where Daph had parked for the football match, and Erin noticed the signs pointing the way to the ground. Ever since the evening Brad had explained his feelings about football, whenever anything associated with the game came up, she did her best to distract his attraction.

'You don't have to do that, you know,' he said, giving her a mock frown.

'What?'

'I caught you! Standing between me and the Carrow Road sign so I don't have to see it.'

'But I . . . ' She stopped. What was the point in pretending.

'I'm not going to burst into tears or run off screaming, you know! You really don't have to keep walking on eggshells the whole time. It'd be unbearable for the both of us.' Smiling, he leaned forwards and brushed her lips softly. 'But I love you for being so thoughtful and considerate.'

To hide her pleasure and confusion, Erin made a bit of a song and dance about getting Walt into the back seat of Metal Mickey. The collie jumped in and settled down on the rug straight away and gave her a look as if to ask what all the fuss was about.

'He's used to travelling,' Brad said. 'He must have done it in the past.'

'Aren't you curious,' she asked, behind the wheel and heading out of the city centre, 'about what sort of life he had before?'

'Desperately, but there's just no way of knowing. He wasn't micro-chipped, the vets checked. I suspect he was dumped.'

'Ouch.' She winced. 'That's just horrible.'

Erin peeked in the rear-view mirror. Walt was sitting upright, peering quietly out of the side window. It was difficult to equate such a sorry background with the animal he was now.

'He's such a love, isn't he? I can see why you fell for him and didn't want to let him go to a shelter.'

'I'm a pushover for a pair of soulful brown eyes. However,' he added, squeezing his hand over hers on the gear stick, 'I quite like green ones, too!'

She laughed. How did he know she'd been wondering if hers might have the same effect. And he'd said he loved her — or almost, hadn't he?

'Do you really not mind quite so much now, Brad, about the football thing? What's changed?'

'Not sure.' He shrugged. 'Growing up? Growing older?'

'Oh, you poor old thing!' she murmured.

Brad was quiet for a second or two, before looking at her meaningfully and adding, 'And other things to think about now.'

Reaching Brundenham, they decided to have lunch at the Rosy Leaf, sitting at one of the outside tables. Nearly everyone who passed stopped to make a fuss of Walt.

Rosie, after serving them two bowls

of lasagne, returned with a third bowl.

'For Walt. Some offcuts from tonight's beef joint.'

'More like prime cuts!' Brad peeped into the bowl just before Walt made short work of the contents.

'He's a lovely dog,' Rosie said. 'You could keep him upstairs if you wanted, you know.'

'That's really good of you, Rosie. But not very practical, what with no garden and downstairs being a food establishment.' He glanced at Erin. 'And I rather think Erin's quite keen to have him now.'

'Oh, well.' Rosie sighed. 'Alternatively, I could just take him home to live with me! We're planning on getting a dog, Oliver and I, when we retire, you know.'

Brad made a fuss of Walt after Rosie had gone back inside.

'You're proving very popular, my boy! I didn't know Rosie had any retirement plans, though,' he mused to Erin.

'No, she and Oliver and the café seem to be a fixed part of the village,

don't they? Unthinkable of Brundenham without them and the Rosy Leaf.'

Was Brad also reflecting on how it
could affect him with regards to the
upstairs bedsit? But then he would
probably have moved out long before
any sale of the premises went through.
And so might she, Erin realised with a
jolt. She might very well be back in her
high-rise city flat, rejoining the ranks of
the nine-to-sixes in a twenty-four-seven
world, leaving behind everything she'd
come to love.

'If you can hang on to the bedsit until
March, then Owl Cottage will be
available.' She covered the crack in her
voice with a cough. And the shiver that
went through her was only in part due
to the cloud that temporarily hid the
sun and shaded the street.

'It's chilly when the sun goes in,'
Brad said gruffly, leaping to his feet.
'Shall we warm up with a walk? Walt's
keen to explore his new surroundings.'

'Yes, let's. Come on, Walt!' Erin, too,
shot to her feet, determined to push

away sour thoughts of her uncertain future and to simply enjoy the present. Gorgeous countryside, gorgeous dog — and gorgeous Brad. Surely that was more than enough to be going on with for now.

After a few skirmishes with the cats to begin with, Walt settled down happily in Owl Cottage. It took a bit of furniture-rearranging to accommodate his new basket in the tiny sitting-room. In no way was a dog an interior design feature, but there was no denying that the addition of Walt had given the cottage a homelier, cosier feel. The cats nearly always drifted up to her when she returned home, but with Walt, the welcome was instantaneous and effusive.

There was also the added benefit of Brad spending a lot more evenings at Owl Cottage.

'You'll tell me if you get fed up with me round here all the time?'

When he said things like that, she discovered how it was possible to love someone very much — as she was sure now that she did — yet still be exasperated by them at the same time. Didn't he know by now that his company never palled? That an evening without him felt incomplete?

And then came an even worse thought; if it were not for Walt, would he not call by so frequently?

There was also still the football issue that had never been completely resolved. Brad's sensitivity had lessened considerably, enough for Erin not to consciously avoid the subject.

But she thought it was a shame that he'd cut himself off from a sport he'd once been so involved in. He said he was happy with his accounts work for the hotel, but she still noted that lost and distant look about his eyes sometimes. And although it was a relief to know that his ex-girlfriend wasn't the cause, she couldn't help thinking that by turning his back so irrevocably on anything to do with the world of football, he was cutting off his nose to spite his face.

'Don't give up on me, Erin,' he'd pleaded, when one of the discussions she'd initiated had ended coolly. 'I'm working on it, OK?'

'Well, if you're arguing,' Elaine was quick to point out in one of their telephone conversations, 'then you've moved on a stage. As long as you make up nicely afterwards and don't end up walloping each other over the head with the saucepans or whatever.'

'Saucepans!' Erin laughed. 'Whatever are they?'

'Still haven't learned to cook, then!' Elaine tutted, referring to Erin's famous lack of culinary skill. 'You'll never become an ideal housewife at this rate!'

'Give me the garden any day.'

Brad was handy in the kitchen. The dishes he created on the small mini-cooker in his bedsit were amazing. More frequently though, he came over to Owl Cottage when he'd finished work, and used her kitchen which, in comparison, was luxuriously spacious.

One evening towards the end of the

month she drove over to Greensides with Walt and waited for Brad to leave off work. They gave Walt a good long run round the perimeter of the grounds that skirted the golf course, before heading back to hers.

'Can we stop at the shop?' he asked, as they approached the village. 'I need some more ingredients for dinner. You're in for a culinary treat tonight.'

'What is it?'

'Just wait and see,' he teased. 'I hope you're not too starving. It might take a while to prepare.'

She was, but Brad's food was worth holding out for.

'I can take my mind off my stomach by doing some advertising for the October Fayre.'

It was a traditional event in the village, held on the Green, and this was to be its sixty-fifth year. As well as designing the advertising, Erin had also offered the organising committee her help with finding sponsors for some of the games and events. While she waited outside the shop in Metal Mickey, Pete Carr drove by, flashing his van's headlamps. Anne Grange, the church volunteer, who was also on the parish committee, stopped on her way past for a few words.

'We're keeping the church open during daylight hours until the clocks go back. There's been that many extra tourists in the village this year! The museum has had its best summer ticket sales ever.'

'The weather's been kind,' Erin commented.

'It's not just the weather,' Anne said, peering down insightfully at Erin over her half-moon glasses. 'I'm convinced it's due to Brundenham's image being raised in all the right ways.'

Erin didn't normally blush at a professional compliment, but this one was close to her heart.

'If it's helped, then I'm thrilled. Once people arrive, the village sells itself, really.'

The trees that lined the main street and the ones in the gardens were just starting to change colour. The air was clear and fresh. The mixture of house styles and rooflines was attractive and appealing.

'Yes, but they have to know we're here in the first place.'

Brad eventually returned from the shop with an overflowing carrier bag, and after a bit more conversation, finally they got moving again.

'Have you noticed,' he remarked, 'how difficult it is in Brundenham to just nip out and do anything?'

'You mean how popping out to post a letter can take an hour, depending on how many people you bump into?'

'Yes.'

'It's great, isn't it?'

They looked at each other and smiled.

Bustling into Owl Cottage, the cats came up for a fussing, Walt bounded clean over them and into the kitchen to his water bowl. Brad unpacked the shopping and began collating the equipment he needed. As he moved about the kitchen cupboards with an easy familiarity, Erin thought how good it was to see him there. She loved their domestic evenings in together.

She put the kettle on to boil, and moved her laptop out of his way and set it up on the coffee table.

'I'll work in here. We can still carry on chatting at the same time.'

'That's the beauty of a tiny cottage,' he said.

Erin noticed the answerphone light was blinking.

'Someone's left me a message.'

'Play it,' Brad urged, pausing in mixing a sauce. 'It might be a job.'

When she pressed the button to play the message, it was Spencer's voice that fractured the silence.

'Erin, I want you back, and on your terms. Call me. Please.'

October Fayre

In the village, the main topic of conversation was the weather. Specifically, whether the Indian Summer would hold until the last Saturday of the month, which was when the October Fayre was held.

'We have the same worry every year,' Daph said.

She was putting the kettle on for Erin and Brad, who'd ended up at the Carrs's bungalow after a Sunday morning run with Walt round the fields. He was flopped out under their kitchen table, but with one eye on the glass oven door, beyond which a joint was roasting.

'Can't think why they don't have it in the summer,' Pete grumbled, breaking the seal on a packet of biscuits. Walt's ears waggled.

'That's no guarantee of good weather,' Daph said.

'And then it wouldn't be an October

Fayre,' Brad pointed out.

'You mean, why not have the Fayre outside of the football league season!' Erin scolded Pete. 'So you don't have to decide between missing the Fayre or missing the game.'

Pete held up his hands and grinned.

'You've got me bang to rights! Actually it's not so difficult a choice this year because City are playing away and I hate the travelling. And the Fayre is my one chance a year to put on the strip, pretend to be Grant Holt and get away with it — all in the name of charity!'

While he was talking Erin caught Daph sneaking a concerned glance at Brad. Brad noticed it, too, and reassured her.

'Don't worry, Daph. Football's no longer entirely a taboo subject. Erin's been working on me.' He gave her a fond glance, which made her stomach flip.

'She's been trying to convince me to get involved in the training side somehow.'

'A work in progress,' Erin said.

Erin was so relieved that the hiatus caused by Spencer's phone call was behind them. She'd discovered, on finally reaching him the following day, it was as an employee that Spencer wanted her back. Erin's replacement hadn't worked out as well as Spencer had anticipated.

'Any personal involvement Spencer and I ever had is long in the past,' she'd told Brad firmly.

If Brad's subtle but cool withdrawal was due to jealousy then Erin could allow herself a spark of hope.

'He's offering you your job back, Erin. If it's not working out for you here as you'd wanted, aren't you tempted to go back?'

'Not in the slightest!'

She was completely certain of that.

'Spencer Riggs is not the only firm in the country. There'll be other jobs around when the time comes.'

In polar opposition to her growing happiness since she'd been based at

Owl Cottage, she'd also been fighting time. It was something she hadn't anticipated when embarking on her leap year, that the ticking clock would feel like a giant pendulum swinging above her head. Perhaps that was because she never expected to find such happiness in so short a space of time. She wanted her life here to go on for ever, and as things stood now that just wasn't possible.

But her leap year was far from over yet. Something could turn up between now and the end of February.

Leaving the bungalow and making their way along the main street, they found Rosie washing down the tables and chairs outside the Rosy Leaf.

'Rosie doesn't open for business on Sundays, does she?' Erin marvelled.

Brad shook his head.

'But they sometimes come in and catch up with some of the cleaning.'

'Hey!' Rosie straightened up, easing her back at the same time. 'We've just been talking about you two. Have you got a few moments?'

Rosie came back out with her husband, Oliver, who was carrying a tray of coffee and biscuits.

'Might as well make the most of the weather,' she said.

Erin and Brad exchanged curious glances, wondering what it was all about.

'You know all the extra tourists we've been having lately,' Rosie began when they'd all settled down around a table. 'Well, we've been talking about opening up on Sundays to cater for them.'

'Good idea,' Erin said. 'And you'd get local trade, too.'

'That's what we thought,' Oliver told her. 'We only wish we'd thought of it earlier in the year!'

'Yes, but we have now, and that's the point,' Rosie pointed out. 'What we thought was, trialing it for October, just to see how it goes.'

Brad was nodding thoughtfully.

'Sounds great, but you're working six days and two evenings a week as it is.'

Rosie beamed at them in turn.

'That's where you two come in.' She glanced at Oliver, who gave a small nod. 'We wondered whether you might like to give it a go.'

'Us!'

Erin was shocked. She looked at Brad. He was wide-eyed with surprise, too.

'I don't know the first thing about running a café!'

'I know how to work the coffee machine,' Brad said, who seemed to have recovered more quickly than Erin. 'I gave him a crash course one Saturday morning when I was rushed off my feet.'

'And you're a great cook, Brad,' Oliver commented.

'Which would make you great in the kitchen, while Erin would be a natural in front-of-house with the customers.' Rosie beamed at her.

'Weren't they thinking of retiring?' Erin asked, when she and Brad had returned to Owl Cottage to discuss the idea. 'Now they want to extend their opening hours! What do you think?'

'Personally, I'd love to give it a go. But only if you're interested, Erin.'

'I am. Definitely.'

It felt exciting now the shock had worn off. A new challenge, only for the month, and Rosie and Oliver would be at the end of the phone should any disaster or problem strike.

'Let's do it, then.' Brad looked as eager as she felt. 'We'll pop back down the Rosy Leaf and let them know our verdict.'

Rosie and Oliver were delighted with their decision, and their enthusiasm. They gave Erin and Brad a quick run through what was involved and how things worked. They also discussed the financial arrangement. It was basically that, whatever money they took, after deducting the cost of the ingredients, they would keep.

'That seems really generous,' Erin mused, thinking about all the hidden service costs.

'It needs to be worth your while,' Oliver said, 'and we'll benefit in the longer run with the café being open for longer. It creates more of a buzz about the place, somehow.' Erin knew what he meant. Anyone finding a café closed, for whatever reason, was less likely to return to see if it was open another time. And the money which she and Brad would hopefully make would come in handy. Particularly with so little coming in from her consultancy work.

But the top attraction for Erin was the thought of spending time working alongside Brad. It would be interesting to see how they worked as a team. She could also daydream that they were the new Rosie and Oliver, husband and wife team of the Rosy Leaf.

She caught herself up sharply. That was a fantasy too far. She doubted she'd have the time for daydreaming when customers needed serving and she was rushed off her feet.

'I'll come in during the week for a

shift, if that's all right, Rosie,' Erin said. 'Just so I can get a feel of it while you're around to keep an eye on me.'

Brad would be working at the hotel from Monday to Friday as usual, but he was confident with what he'd be doing in the kitchen.

'All right for you,' she teased, 'behind the scenes and no-one to see if anything goes wrong. Make a fool of myself out front, and it'll be in public view!'

'You'll be great at it,' Brad told her enthusiastically.

'What, making a fool of myself?'

It was a busy week, thinking about the café on Sunday, and Erin also had advertising and other arrangements to finalise for the October Fayre.

Then Pete Carr rang with a problem. 'You know the five-a-side footie for the Fayre?'

She did. And she knew it was a popular fixture in the programme of events. Teams from all over the district entered. It was fun, but the trophy was hotly contested. Pete headed one of the

Brundenham Teams, comprising him, his son and three other village men, one of whom had now had to pull out at the last minute.

'He can't get the time off work. I'm in a right fix, Erin. Everyone else who can play is already in a team.'

'And if you scratch your team, it'll put the draw system right out, won't it?' Erin tapped her teeth with a pen.

'There's no way I'm scratching,' Pete said emphatically. 'Not that we have much chance of winning, but I've led out the Carrbines team ever since my lad was born.'

Erin heard Pete draw his breath in, and wondered what was coming.

'So why I'm ringing is, to ask you whether Brad might consider playing for us.'

'Oh!' she exclaimed. 'Well, there's only one way to find out, Pete. That's to ask him.'

★ ★ ★

'Sure you've got those the right way up?'

She was planting some bulbs in the garden when Brad arrived after work. Walt jumped up the gate to greet him. Erin sat back on her heels and thought that this was what it would be like if they were a proper couple. Except he'd also run over, lift her to her feet and kiss her thoroughly.

There'd been a few more kisses since that first light one, but they'd all been casual and fleeting. Her fears that Brad would continue putting up a wall to getting deeply involved again after Jenna were proving frustratingly accurate.

True to form, rather than rushing to kiss her now, he wandered over and picked up the bulb wrapper instead. He frowned.

'Hey, it says they'll flower next April. You won't be here to see them, will you?'

Erin resumed digging narrow holes so he couldn't see the disappointment on her face.

'Probably not, but whoever is living here will get the pleasure.'

It might even be him, she added silently to herself. Because anything else more suitable to rent had yet to come up. And if she wasn't able to continue living in Owl Cottage after February, if she had to go back to the city, then the thought of Brad being here gave her some comfort. Perhaps she could even come over and visit some time? But no. He'd probably have a girlfriend by then. Pain cut through at her at that thought.

When they were out together she'd seen women look at him in an interested way, even if Brad never seemed to notice. But once he was fully over the disappointments of his past, he'd be ready for a serious permanent relationship eventually. Even if it wasn't going to be with her.

And why couldn't it be with her? Because she looked a bit like the treacherous Jenna? Or was there some other reason?

'Penny for them?' Brad said softly.

Blinking, Erin got to her feet and decided it was as good a time as any to sound him out about Pete's five-a-side plea.

As she'd expected, his first reaction was to refuse. Putting on football boots again was a long way removed from talking about the game, or even discussing the idea of getting involved in some non-playing capacity.

But his initial refusal was nowhere near as vehement as she'd feared. It gave her hope that he might be persuaded. She didn't want to offend him by arguing that, as part of a fun five-a-sider, no-one expected any great things from the participants anyway. But she was concerned about how playing again might affect his old injuries.

'They wouldn't stop me having a run about on the Green,' he said thoughtfully. 'As long as the opposition didn't play too dirty!'

'I'd say you're fit enough.'

Erin glancing ruefully at Walt. She sometimes wondered whether the dog had been a greyhound in a previous life! Despite his lazy looks, once he was off the lead he had a fair turn of foot. She couldn't keep up with him, and when Walt was in one of his determined pursuits of a rabbit or a squirrel, it was Brad who sprinted fast enough to catch him before he disappeared altogether.

'I might pop down and see Pete, have a chat about it. Have a bit of a kick about in their back garden. I'm so out of practice.'

Erin was thrilled that he was prepared to consider it. She couldn't resist going up and throwing her arms around his neck, pulling him close to her.

'Hey!' he exclaimed, looking delightedly down at her.

She loved being in his arms. She wished he knew how deeply she felt for him. More to the point, she wished she knew how he really felt about her.

* * *

Their first Sunday at the café was exhausting. Erin had expected it to be hard work, but with it being the Rosy Leaf's first-ever Sunday opening, she'd convinced herself that trade would be manageably slow.

How wrong she'd been. With the weather holding, there were still plenty of tourists and day trippers dropping in. Plus Erin had underestimated the village's own communication system. Once one local person discovered they were open, the news was quickly all round Brundenham, and one set of familiar faces after another called in. All the chatting and explaining slowed down the serving process, but no-one minded waiting and Erin was grateful for everyone's support.

'I hope this isn't just the novelty factor,' she said to Brad as she zipped around the kitchen, preparing trays and plating up the lunchtime snacks he was preparing. 'Next Sunday, we might be empty.'

'I don't think so,' he said, checking

on the row of toasting baguettes under the grill. 'I think it shows there's a real need. We're offering an alternative to pub grub, and in a more traditional setting.'

'If this keeps up,' Erin said, conscious that the door bell was ringing with more new customers, 'we'll have to think about employing someone to help.'

If it got too much, Rosie and Oliver had promised to be only a phone call away, but Erin was adamant that they wouldn't trouble them — well, only in a dire emergency.

Brad felt the same.

'They deserve a day off, and anyway, I like the idea of a challenge. We can prove to ourselves we can do it on our own.'

By the afternoon, with her legs feeling more and more as if they were filled with concrete, Erin was wondering if they had bitten off more than they could chew.

'Want to swap?' Brad offered, holding out a wooden spoon. 'I don't mind taking a turn at the tables.'

Erin took one look at the sauce he was making for his own hand-made pizza bases, and shook her head fearfully.

'Me and sauces don't seem to gel.'

Brad gave a mock groan.

'You can't be too tired. You're making puns!'

'Unintentionally.' She grinned. 'Anyway, I'd like to keep going for a bit longer. Daph and Pete have just sat down. I'll take them some of these.' She began loading up a tray with some of Brad's recent creations.

'This all looks fabulous!' a wide-eyed Daph exclaimed as Erin served her and Pete with a large plate of cake and pastries. 'It's like a proper, old-fashioned afternoon tea, only a more posh version. Did Brad make all of these?'

Erin nodded proudly.

'I know you said he could cook, Erin, but he's been hiding his light under a bushel, good and proper!'

Pete's hand was hovering between

the cupcakes, the Bakewell slices and the mini gateaux.

'I wish I hadn't had such a big lunch now.'

'Not that that will stop him.' Daph grinned. 'What did I tell you?' She gasped as Pete helped himself to one of each. 'Don't forget you're supposed to be in training for the five-a-side.'

'Well, what about you?' Pete retorted, looking pointedly at the jam and cream-covered scone that Daph was about to demolish.

After two more Sundays, Erin felt she was getting the hang of the café trade, and finding it increasingly enjoyable as she got to grips with everything. With Brad's food proving so popular, the customers kept on coming.

'Just one more Sunday left to go,' Erin said as the end of the month drew close.

She was going to miss it. And it was going to be a shorter day, too, because the clocks were due to go back on the Saturday night, so they were closing at four instead of five.

'We might be glad of it,' Brad remarked. 'You haven't forgotten what we're doing on Saturday?'

Saturday was the October Fayre and the long anticipated five-a-side tournament.

'Forgotten it? I've hardly thought about anything else.' Apart from helping out with the organisational side, she'd also rashly agreed to play for Daph's Ducklings in the ladies' five-a-side tournament.

Brad had been coaching her.

'You're either terribly brave or a glutton for punishment,' she told him when he first offered. She'd never played football in her life. 'The nearest I've ever come to it was being substitute for my school hockey team.'

'It's not that different really, but just remember you don't carry a stick!'

'It's completely different. I never even got off the bench at hockey!'

He stood in a tracksuit with his hands parked either side of his waist and gave her a stern look.

'Come on. Less chatting, more training!'

'Yes, sir!'

Brad started her off by showing her how to dribble the ball. The long back garden of Owl Cottage was serving as an impromptu training ground. They could have gone to the Green, but Erin had said it was bad enough making an idiot of herself in front of him, let alone half the village. That would happen soon enough at the Fayre.

But what with Napoleon and all four of his ladies stopping pecking to stare, plus the astonished faces of Feather and Mouse who'd come out to watch, and then Walt joined in thinking it was a game for his benefit, the Green might have been marginally less busy.

'The others are still looking at me!' Erin wailed after Walt had been lured indoors with a biscuit and a promise of a game with him afterwards.

'There'll be more than just chickens and cats eyes on you on Saturday,' he said, with a gleam in his eye which made her legs wobble.

Unless it was just her muscles protesting from the unaccustomed exercise!

On the morning of the tournament, Erin tied up her hair, pulled on her new sports' jogging bottoms and a T-shirt, got into Metal Mickey and drove down to pick Brad up from the Rosy Leaf.

He emerged wearing a silver-grey track suit and professional-looking football boots.

'I could never bear to part with them,' he said quietly when he got into the passenger seat and saw her noticing his feet. 'I never thought I'd ever be wearing them again.'

The break in his voice affected her deeply.

'Brad, will you give me a hug?'

He turned awkwardly in the car across the gear stick, and drew her to him.

'What for?'

'Because I'm feeling scared,' she

mumbled into his chest.

'You needn't be,' he said, smoothing her hair, and making her wish they were driving off somewhere quiet and intimate, just the two of them. 'You'll be fine.'

At that moment, she didn't much bother whether she fell flat on her face or not. But she couldn't let him know what was really troubling her.

It was the thought of Brad going back on the pitch again. How would it affect him? And that was the real point of asking for a hug. She'd wanted to give him a big hug, but had been scared a show of sympathy might scare him off.

'This is lovely,' he mumbled into her hair. 'But not only have several people just walked by with raised eyebrows, we also need to get over to the Green.'

Reluctantly, Erin drew back, and with a very pink face she turned the ignition key.

Brundenham's village green was surrounded by trees that had turned the most glorious autumnal shades of gold, amber and auburn. They made a picturesque backdrop to the area that was packed with marquees, stalls and lots and lots of people. A loud tannoy system was already in operation, guiding motorists into the car park, and later it would be announcing each event in turn.

After leaving the car, Brad and Erin made their way to the centre, walking through gently cascading leaves that the faintest of breezes had disturbed.

They found Pete in one of the tents, already rallying his team, The Carrbines.

'Great, we're all here now.' Pete welcomed Brad with a look of relief, and introduced him to the others.

It had already been agreed that Pete wasn't going to mention Brad's professional past to the others, but the way a couple of the Carrbines looked at him suggested to Erin that they either recognised him or that his name rang a bell.

Pete handed out a tabard for each of

his team. Typically they were yellow and green.

'It's the only way I'm ever going to play in the Canaries strip!' He grinned ruefully.

'Are you OK?' Erin couldn't help asking Brad, raking his expression for clues.

He squeezed her hands.

'I think so. Don't worry, Erin. I'm just going to get out there and get on with it. Wish me luck.'

She reached up on tiptoe and kissed him full and hard on the mouth.

'All the luck in the world.'

Drawing back, looking slightly astonished, he breathed in to speak, but then Pete was pulling him away.

'Come on, lads, we're on!'

Erin watched the Carrbines jog over to their marked quarter of the full-sized pitch, but she was only really focusing on one of them. She wasn't able to detect any sign of a limp or weakness in Brad's legs, but she'd earlier caught sight of scars running down both calves, and particularly around the knees.

Daph was suddenly at her elbow. Thank goodness, Erin thought, clutching her arm for support as she watched Brad. The referee had blown the whistle and the Carrbines had kicked off. It was only ten minutes each half, but she was terrified the whole time.

'I don't think you've got much to worry about there,' Daph said. 'Brad looks in his element, doesn't he?'

Erin nodded in relief. And when it came to playing the ball even she, with her woeful lack of knowledge on the subject, could see the different skill level between Brad and everyone else.

'Oh, my gosh, yes!' Daphne shrieked. 'Look, he's only gone and scored!'

They both jumped up and down screamed with joy, but Erin was by far the loudest. She didn't care what anyone thought. She only realised how loud she'd been when she caught Brad peering across with a concerned expression. Then he gave her a huge grin and a thumbs-up sign.

When the Carrbines trotted off, the 4-2 winners of their first-round match, the tannoy was already announcing the start of the women's tournament. Erin, Daph and the other three women in the team had to dash to the changing area in another tent.

'I'll be watching,' Brad called after her. 'Good luck, Erin. Good luck, the Ducklings!' He pulled a face. 'Ducklings, but far from ugly.'

'Thanks, Brad, but reserve judgement on that until after you've seen us play!' Daph replied.

'Yeah, good luck, gal!' Pete gave his wife a fond tap on her not inconsiderable bottom. 'Go show 'em what you're made of.'

'That's what I'm worried about,' Daph quipped to Erin.

In her bright yellow tabard, Erin jogged nervously on to the pitch with the rest of the team. The whistle blew, and the rest was a bit of a blur.

The game was fast and furious. They

seemed to be doing OK in keeping the ball away from the opposition, but in the dying seconds of the second half, a tall thin girl weaved through the Ducklings' defence, and slipped the ball past a goalkeeping Daph. The Ducklings were out first round, one-nil.

'Never mind,' Pete consoled them — Daph in particular — when they'd traipsed over to the sidelines. 'It was your first try. Better luck next year.'

'Yeah, next year!' The Ducklings high-fived cheerily, and Erin joined in. But next year, she thought with a suddenly overwhelming crushing dismay, she probably wouldn't be in Brundenham.

'Don't be down-hearted, Erin. You did fantastically well,' Brad said, giving her a hug. 'I watched you out there and I was so proud of my girl!'

Was she really his girl?

There was no time for any more chat. The Carrbines next game was imminent. Erin stood at the edge of the pitch and cheered them on during the next four rounds. Brad scored another two goals, after both of which Erin yelled herself hoarse.

But finally Pete's Carrbines were knocked out in the semi-finals by a nearby village team that had been playing together in similar tournaments for years.

'So absolutely no shame in losing to them,' Pete pronounced breathlessly.

'He's exhausted anyway, bless him!' Daph winked at Erin. 'I think he's relieved it's over for another year.'

'How do you feel?' Erin asked Brad.

It was unnecessary; his face was alight in a way she'd never seen before.

'I'm whacked. I'm out of breath. I'm happy,' he said. 'I've never been happy about losing a game before, but this is different. Erin, you got me to this place . . .'

He pulled her to him, and then he was kissing her. The kiss she'd longed for; deep, meaningful, purposeful. It went on and on. It was only when Pete gave an exaggerated cough that they pulled apart. Erin's face was blazing, but she still couldn't stop smiling.

'Do you want to stop for the final?' Brad whispered in her ear. No longer pressed together, but his arm was curled firmly around the shoulders.

'We'd better,' she replied, but more than hopeful that he'd contradict her. 'It might look unsporting if we didn't. Wouldn't it?'

'Yes, I suppose it would.' He was sighing as he said it. 'Let's hope they get a move on, then.'

Erin felt a shiver of anticipation at the prospect of them being alone together.

When the event was over and they could leave, Erin went to fetch her bag, which had been left with one of the volunteers in the admin marquee. As she fished for the car keys, she came across her phone.

It wasn't some sixth sense that forewarned her. She'd been on alert for a call for the last few days, since Elaine had said she'd been having twinges.

'A missed call,' she told Brad,

glancing at the screen. 'I bet it's from Elaine telling me she's booking herself into hospital!'

But when she checked properly, there were half-a-dozen missed calls, and they were all from Graham's phone. She turned to Brad with icy fear filling her veins.

'Something must be wrong.'

Brad grabbed her hand and they ran for the car. He drove while she tried to reach Graham.

'It's going straight to voicemail!' she said, throwing the phone down into the footwell.

'Leave a message, then,' Brad advised. 'He'll get back to you when he can.'

Brad, she discovered, was calm and logical in a crisis. He drove back to Owl Cottage, and told her to pack a bag, while he checked out the train times to Manchester. He knew she didn't trust Metal Mickey on that sort of trip.

Then finally her phone rang. Erin snatched it up.

'Graham! What's happening?'

'She's in hospital. They've stabilised

her. They might have to do a Caesarean. We've got to wait and see.'

It wasn't just the words, but his clipped voice, that told her how scared he was, and how serious it was.

'I'm on my way over now,' she told him.

'What about the boys?' Brad asked as they were on the way to the railway station at Norwich.

'They're with Graham's mum.' Erin was distracted, her mind turning over the practicalities now. Walt, the cats, the chickens.

'I'll stay at Owl Cottage, like we said, and keep everyone and everything ticking over. So don't worry about anything this end.'

'Use the car to get to work,' she said, glad that she'd had the foresight to add Brad to the insurance policy.

Erin had planned this trip to Manchester after the baby was born, so they had already discussed the arrangements, but she wasn't expecting it to be in a panic like this.

Her hand flew to her mouth.

'What about Rosy Leaf tomorrow? It's supposed to be our last opening Sunday.'

'I'd already sounded out Claire. She said she wouldn't mind earning a few extra quid if we ever needed help. I don't think she's got a shift at Greensides tomorrow.'

'Claire? Oh, yes.' Erin couldn't place her for a second, then of course she could. Claire was the bright and breezy hotel receptionist. 'Yes, she'd be ideal.'

She glanced anxiously at Brad.

He squeezed her hand.

'Don't worry. She won't replace you! No-one could ever do that.'

Erin felt like crying. How could she be so worried about Elaine, yet at the same time feel so jealous about someone else spending time with Brad.

And the answer hit her in a flash. She knew, with complete and utter certainty, that she was totally and irrevocably in love with Brad Cavill.

November Apart

Elaine and Graham's baby daughter was delivered safely on November 2.

'Seven pounds and five ounces,' Erin proudly related down the phone to Brad. 'Mother and baby both doing well.'

'Dad exhausted!' Graham bellowed over her shoulder.

'I'll bet.' Brad's voice had a smile in it. 'How's the aunt?'

'Huh?'

'Aunt Erin. You!'

'Oh! Sorry, Brad, my brain's still shot at the moment. I'm happy.' She laughed. 'Very, very happy.'

'I can hear it,' he said. 'Send my love to all.'

'I will, Brad, thanks.' She ended the call, and wondered if Brad's love to all included her.

'You should have asked him, you

dope!' Elaine said from her hospital bed.

'You're recovering fast!' Erin remarked.

'Thank goodness for that.' Elaine reached for her dressing-gown and eased her feet into her slippers. 'I can't wait to get home and into my own bed. This one might as well be a wooden plank!'

'Your coach awaits, madam!' Graham pushed a wheelchair into the room. Erin gently lifted the baby from the crib, and they all proceeded down the corridor. The doors at the dayroom burst open, and in ran William and Jamie, closely followed by Graham's mum.

'Steady now, boys!' she warned.

But there was no stopping them. They couldn't wait to hug their mum, and see their new baby sister.

'What's her name, Mummy?' William demanded to know, and when Elaine said she didn't yet have one, both boys were astonished.

'See?' Graham said. 'I told you we should have chosen one by now.'

'At least she arrived too early to be a Catherine Wheel.' Elaine pulled a face. 'It's not Guy Fawkes until tomorrow.'

'She must have a name, Mummy!' Jamie protested. 'Everyone's got to have one. I know! It'll be above her peg. Just ask Miss Watson when we go back after half term. She writes out the little labels. She'll know!'

He looked up confidently, surprised to find that everyone was laughing.

★   ★   ★

'King Arthur's grown,' Erin remarked as she swung a cotton-reel on a length of string to amuse the kitten that was now very nearly a fully grown cat.

'Hasn't he just!' Elaine replied. 'He was only a prince when he left you.'

'It's been lovely spending a few days with you all.'

Erin sighed. She was torn between enjoying this short spell with her family, and itching to get back to Norfolk at the same time.

'But you're missing Brad and need to get back.' Elaine smiled knowledgeably as she sipped her coffee. 'I've not been married so long that I can't remember first love! It's not called lovesick for nothing.'

'There's work, too,' Erin reminded her, reminding herself at the same time. What image consultancy work there was around . . .

'I've been looking through our family box,' Elaine said.

'Do we have such a thing?'

'I put it together when I had my family tree phase and ordered all those old certificates. Anyway, I discovered our great-grandmother was born on November the second.'

'Crikey. How long ago was that?'

'Oh, eighteen-hundred and something. But I thought it might be nice to use the name again.'

'Hmm,' Erin nodded cautiously. 'But as long as it's not Ermentrude or Euphemia or something!'

'It's Beatrice. Me and Graham both

like it. What do you think?'

'Beatrice. Oh, it's lovely.' Erin crept softly over to the sleeping baby. 'Beatrice,' she whispered. 'It really suits her. Oh, you're so lucky, Elaine.'

'It'll be your turn soon. Just see if I'm not right. You and Brad.'

Erin puffed out her cheeks incredulously.

'I can't see how it can possibly work out in the long run.'

'Just wait and see. If it's written in the stars, it's meant to be.'

Erin pulled a face at her sister.

'Are you still suffering the effects of gas and air?'

'Probably. Do you want to know Beatrice's second name?'

'It's Turner, isn't it?'

Elaine spluttered and rolled her eyes.

'Yes, it's Beatrice Turner, of course. But it's Beatrice Erin Turner.'

'Oh!' Erin exclaimed, staring at her sister. 'Oh,' she repeated, feeling herself welling up.

Erin dozed fitfully on the train

journey back to Norfolk. Every time the train rattled, she woke, imagining she must be there, but it was only a few miles further than the last time she checked. It had been wonderful, spending a week with everyone, helping Elaine and getting to know her new niece, Beatrice Erin. The name still gave her a thrill. She was going to be her godmother, too, at the christening in the spring.

But Erin's main desire now was to get back to Owl Cottage. She couldn't wait to see Feather and Mouse, Napoleon and the girls. And Walt.

And Brad, of course. Most of all, it was him.

She caught sight of her reflected face in the huge window. She was grinning to herself like an idiot. What on earth must the other passengers think? But they were lost in their own worlds, so Erin went back to hers.

She'd missed Brad like crazy. On the phone, he'd said he missed her. She couldn't wait to see him again, be in his arms, and pick up where they'd left off after that kiss at the October Fayre. How many times had she relived that perfect kiss since then?

She had to change trains twice. Hold ups, maintenance on the line, then the engine broke down altogether and they were stuck for half an hour in the middle of nowhere.

Finally she arrived back at Thorpe Station, feeling rattled, hungry and grubby. It was just gone half-past four, and the rain was lashing down. Rather than call Brad away from work to drive across to Norwich to collect her, she decided to get a taxi. She reckoned she'd arrive at Owl Cottage about the same time as he got back from work.

When the taxi pulled up, Metal Mickey was already parked outside the gate and the downstairs lights were switched on. She felt a rush of love for the cottage, and for everyone inside. Brad would be surprised to see her; she hadn't even told him she was coming back today.

She paid off the taxi. The driver handed out her suitcase, and sped away.

It was only then she noticed the other car parked bumper to bumper with hers. It was a vaguely familiar looking silver Audi. Suddenly it came to her. It was Spencer's car.

What on earth was he doing here? The bonnet was still warm; she touched it as she passed. With the rain plastering her hair to her skull and drips pouring down her neck of her mac, she scuttled up the path and hesitantly opened the door.

Both men looked up. Brad was leaning by the kitchen doorway, looking absolutely gorgeous in cord trousers and a chunky green sweater. Spencer was sitting on the edge of the sofa.

Walt bounded over Spencer's well-tailored legs to greet her. Erin dropped down and buried her face in his fur. It wasn't quite the romantic 'welcome home' scenario with Brad that she'd had in mind all through her journey. But Walt was definitely the next best thing. Then the cats wanted a fussing.

Erin wanted Brad. Why wasn't he saying anything? She lifted her face to look at him, but Spencer, who was closer, caught her attention first by standing up.

'Hello, Erin. Brad was just telling me he didn't know when he was expecting you.'

Erin glanced at Brad momentarily.

'No, I didn't tell him I was coming back today. It was going to be a surprise.'

Some surprise. Shock, more like, and she'd been the one to receive it. She had no idea why she was explaining this to Spencer; it was nothing to do with him.

She shook her head, trying to lift the fog.

'Why are you here, anyway?'

'To talk you into coming back.'

'But I told you last month, I'm not coming.'

She wondered how she could get over to Brad, without brushing past Spencer.

She gazed at Brad, hoping he'd realise her predicament and come over to her.

He straightened up, but stayed where he was.

'You're soaked, Erin,' he said with calm concern. 'And you must be exhausted. I'll make some coffee and sandwiches while you two talk.'

He turned and headed into the kitchen.

'No!' Erin wanted to scream.

She wanted Spencer to leave, so she and Brad could talk. This was all wrong. Brad had gone cold again; she could read it in his eyes. Heaven alone only knew what Spencer had been telling him; if he really wanted her back to work for him, there was no-one better than him for putting the right spin on a situation.

'Black for me!' Spencer called out casually, as if totally unaware of the tension in the room.

The woodburner was crackling away merrily, but Erin felt icy cold. Spencer was bouncing his car keys in the palm of his hand, a clear sign to Erin that he was irritated even before he spoke.

'Erin, this is plain crazy. If I'd known you were in Manchester, I wouldn't have had to drive all the way over here.'

'Why on earth should you have known?'

He was making it sound as if she usually kept him informed of her movements.

'And I still don't understand why you did,' she snapped, peeling off her wet coat.

Brad re-emerged quietly with a towel for her hair. He reached around Spencer to pass it to her, but he didn't look at her. He went back into the kitchen.

'If I'd called you up, you'd have just said no,' Spencer went on. 'A face-to-face meeting often brings the best result.'

In business perhaps, she thought.

'It won't this time. I'm sorry you've had a wasted journey, but I don't want to come back to work for you, and that's my last word on the subject.' She really hoped Brad was listening to this.

Spencer gave her a lazy smile.

'You haven't heard why I've actually come yet.'

Erin blinked in bewilderment.

'I'm not offering you a job on the payroll, because you've made it clear you're not interested in coming back until your year here is over.'

Erin opened her mouth to say she couldn't bear the thought of ever going back, but then Spencer went on.

'You're a freelance consultant now. I want to engage your services for a specific contract. After all, is your business really doing so well that you can turn a job down?'

He made it sound as if he already knew the answer. And unfortunately so did Erin.

Brad brought through two mugs of coffee and a plate of sandwiches and put them down on the coffee table. Erin gazed at him, desperately wanting him to intervene. How and with what suggestion, though, she couldn't imagine. She supposed what she longed for was for him to hold her tight, and show Spencer the door. But Brad just wasn't the caveman sort. It was because of the qualities that he did possess that she'd fallen for him, anyway. His modesty and sensitivity and level-headedness.

'Worth hearing him out?' He shrugged to Erin now.

And of course he was right. She'd never had any major rift with Spencer, over business or in their personal relationship. They'd never been close enough for that. She and Spencer had just drifted in different directions, wanting different things.

'I need you for the Easyplease Foods account,' Spencer said.

'Ah.'

Easyplease Foods was a ready-meal manufacturer who she'd done a tremendous amount of successful work with in the past. They were also Spencer Riggs's most significant and high-profile client.

'They've had a recent PR disaster on their hands. A rogue employee spread malicious lies over the internet about poor production techniques, which then reached the local press all over the north and west. The employee has been dealt with, corrections and apologies published, but the company image has suffered and they've asked us to step in again. But they're insisting on you, Erin. If they can't have you, I don't get the business.'

Erin swallowed hard, her mind computing. The money she could earn would enable her to keep afloat independently for several more months. But the price to pay would be going back to Manchester to manage the project from the company's headquarters there.

'When would I need to start?' she asked with a sinking heart, already knowing what the answer would be. With Spencer it was always yesterday.

'Drive back tonight, crack straight on in the morning.'

'But I've only just got back!' she protested.

She looked longingly at Brad, who was loitering in the kitchen. She just wanted Spencer gone, and to sink into Brad's arms.

'I need to discuss this with Brad,' she told Spencer. 'There's all the practicalities to sort out.'

Spencer's mouth opened to protest, but then Erin saw him glance round the cottage, taking in the cats, the dog, and then Brad. He nodded grudgingly.

'OK, I'll wait out in the car.'

He stepped over her suitcase.

'You won't even need to pack!'

Immediately the front door had closed she flew to the kitchen.

'What do you think, Brad?'

Brad leaned against the sink. Behind him, through the window, the night was black, the rain lashing against the glass.

'It's a job, Erin.'

'Wouldn't you mind me going?'

'I'd rather you didn't have to, but I can see why you can't turn it down.'

Erin clenched her teeth. Earlier, she had been appreciating his qualities. Now she was infuriated by them. Did he have to be so measured and reasonable?

'Would you rather I take you in my arms and beg you not to go?'

'Yes!'

She couldn't help smiling. He made it sound so melodramatic.

She stepped forward and leaned against his chest.

'I was looking forward so much to coming home, being with you this evening.'

'I would have been, too, if I'd known that was what you were intending!'

'So much for a surprise! Would you really not mind if I had to work in Manchester for a while?'

'I think I'd mind like crazy,' he said, sending her heart soaring.

He kissed her, with all the strength and passion of the October kiss.

'How long would you be gone?' he asked eventually.

'Not sure. Couple of weeks? A month?'

He groaned.

Short-term pain for longer-term gain, she was thinking. A month away now would mean her being able to stay possibly right through to next summer. That was if the cottage was available. She must check that out with the agent. And then more local work might turn up.

The sound of an impatient car horn made her jump.

'If I'm going, I suppose I might as well let him know,' she said reluctantly. 'And then pack a few extra things before starting off. It's a long trip.'

The thought was incredibly unappealing.

He nodded glumly.

'Where will you stay? With Graham's mother again?'

Erin nodded. Elaine's old spare room was now the new nursery.

She stroked Brad's face.

'I'll be thinking of you the whole time.'

'You'd better put some thought to

the job!' he said. 'Otherwise you'll be back here before you know where you are!'

'And then it really would be only until the end of February,' she muttered.

Brad turned around and started pouring water into the sink to wash the mugs. Erin turned the other way to head upstairs. Walt stood in her path, looking up at her with huge uncertain eyes, his tail swinging doubtfully. She stroked his head, knowing exactly how he felt.

Seated beside Spencer as the car glided smoothly away, Erin felt thoroughly miserable. She turned to gaze out of the side window for the very last view of Brad possible. He stood on the doorstep of Owl Cottage, one hand raised in farewell, the other holding on to Walt's collar. Feather was on the window-sill, with Mouse squeezed in beside her.

And she didn't even get to see Napoleon and his wives, Erin realised.

December Reunion

Spencer had predicted on the journey over to Manchester, that once she was back in her right environment, she'd realise what she'd been missing. Erin had known that all she was missing was back in Norfolk.

Her first morning back, riding the lift up to Spencer's fourth floor office, she felt a strange mixture of déjà vu and nightmare. Everything was exactly the same; the feel of the carpet tiles beneath her feet, the dusty plastic greenery, the claustrophobic atmosphere. It was her who had changed. Changed for good. There was no coming back to this, ever.

Her old colleagues were surprised but pleased to see her walk in, and gathered round her briefly before a look from Spencer sent them scooting back to their desks. Erin caught a rather sour look cross the face of Wendy, the girl who'd rang her to inform her so enjoyably of Erin's replacement. Wendy hadn't called her up to tell her of the new woman's departure, she noted fleetingly.

Not that Erin was interested, nor was she here to participate in office politics.

Spencer clapped his hands and informed everyone that Erin was working with them, not for them, on a temporary basis. Then it was time to leave for the meeting with the Easyplease Foods management team.

Spencer had been wrong about her not needing to pack. She'd nipped up to her bedroom before leaving to add some of her smart business suits, shirts and shoes to her suitcase. Brad was going to stay on at the cottage, continuing the arrangement they'd made to cover her absence while she'd been away for Elaine's baby.

But she'd been unprepared for the strength of sentiment and yearning that had coursed through her as she'd stood at the foot of her iron-framed bed, knowing that Brad had been sleeping in it.

He was very tidy, she'd noted with a smile. The duvet was neatly smoothed out. A deep blue towelling dressing-gown hung from the hook in the bathroom. His toothbrush standing in the rack on the shelf, alongside a shaving razor and a couple of cans of shaving foam and deodorant.

In the wardrobe, a few pairs of work trousers and several crisply ironed shirts hanging next to her skirts and dresses caused another flickering of her heart. As she'd closed the door, the movement of air stirred the faint tang of subtly masculine aftershave that was typical Brad.

Her heart soared with love and longing, and she'd been on the point of overturning her decision and rushing down to tell him she wasn't going. But from outside, a blast of Spencer's car horn had brought her to her senses.

The Easyplease Foods contract was far more complex than she'd expected. She'd no idea of the scale of the disaster until that first meeting with the company representatives.

As they came away, Spencer pointed out testily that if Erin hadn't buried herself away in the country she would have known, and didn't she even bother with the internet nowadays?

It wasn't worth arguing with him. She needed all her energy and ingenuity to deal with the client. It wasn't a case of repairing their image, but completely rebuilding it, and that was going to take time. She had to get up to speed fast.

'It's going to take several weeks,' she told Brad, phoning him rather late at the end of her long and punishing first day. 'Maybe more.'

Liaising with the Press, setting up consumer product review boards, constant meetings with company executives, staff support and re-education programmes, celebrity endorsements, it all took such an inordinate amount of time.

'I remember how time consuming it was at Greensides, and compared with the hotel, Easyplease Foods must be an enormous project to tackle.'

Appreciating his understanding, Erin had been dismayed by it at the same time.

Brad had news for her, too.

'Rosie and Oliver have suggested that the Rosy Leaf carries on with Sunday openings all through November.'

'Oh.'

How would that work out? It definitely wouldn't be practical for her to travel backwards and forwards for the next four Sundays.

'Have you agreed?'

'I said I'd run it by you first. Not so many tourists and visitors about, but local people have got to know we're open, so there's still good trade around. It seems a sound idea to continue, don't you think?'

Yes and no, Erin thought.

'Will Claire help out?' She liked Claire, but had a vision of the bright and bubbly young woman buzzing about the kitchen with Brad, and was stung with jealousy.

Brad chuckled, which made her wonder if he could read her mind.

'Yes, Claire said she'd be happy to earn the extra money. Her boyfriend doesn't mind. He strips down his motorcycle on Sundays apparently.'

Erin had laughed, too, then, with relief.

★ ★ ★

When the time came to turn the office's plain numbered desk calendar to December, Erin briefly imagined herself in the kitchen at Owl Cottage, comparing the photographic calendar on the larder door to the scene from the window. The trees would be black geometric shapes against that mercurial Norfolk sky. The soil, a rich dark brown, rimed with frost on its ploughed ridges.

There might be a couple of deer emerging from the woods. Hardly noticeable on the landscape until they moved, then they'd slowly dissolve away into the background. Her heart ached to see it for real.

It was all so very different from here, where the view from the window was tarmac and traffic, and the only clue to the month was the Christmas displays in the shops.

She'd not been back home once. With Brad working all week at Greensides and Sundays at the Rosy Leaf, and Erin practically working round the clock, it didn't seem to make sense for the amount of time they'd have together.

But mainly she suspected that, if she did go over to Norfolk, she'd never come back to Manchester and finish the job. And if she didn't complete the contract, she wouldn't get paid, which would have made the last month a complete waste of time.

A smaller part of her than usual was taking pride in the way she was helping to rehabilitate Easyplease Foods's tarnished image. It was a revelation to her that, although she was striving as hard as she'd ever done to bring about the best result, her heart was no longer in the work.

As she dashed through traffic and crowds from meeting to meeting, working late under a desk lamp to highlight action plans, write up further proposals, fire off and respond to endless emails, she occasionally paused to reflect back on how she'd felt before opting out of this world for her leap year.

Perhaps she'd just convinced herself that it was only for a year, and it was common sense that told her to keep her options open. Deep down inside, she had always known that this sort of life was no longer for her. What she needed to do when she finally got back to Brundenham was to sit down and work out how she was going to live from now on. At least the contract here would give her a few more months of breathing space.

Apart from the money she was earning, the only other plus of being away from Brad and Owl Cottage was that any free time which could be squeezed from her schedule could be spent with Elaine. It was a real bonus, especially with Christmas coming up fast.

'Much as we'd love you to spend the day with us,' Elaine told Erin with her usual insight, 'I can tell where you'd rather be!'

Erin had her hopes and dreams set on a Christmas Day with Brad and the animals at Owl Cottage. Down to the village in the morning for the service at All Saints', then a walk round the fields with Walt, followed by lunch at the cottage and a cosy afternoon curling up in front of a roaring log fire.

Erin raced like mad against the clock to wind up her work to the client's and Spencer's satisfaction before the holiday started. She managed it with a couple of days to spare. Any loose ends she could now tie up from Norfolk, by phone or e-mail.

'You're really going back?' Spencer asked when she came to clear her temporary desk at the office.

'Back for good.' Perhaps this time, finally, he would accept her decision.

He shook his head.

'I think you're crazy. Is it that chap, Brad?'

She nodded, biting her lip.

Spencer held up his hands.

'If that's what you want, Erin. Thanks for getting me out of a hole. The Easyplease directors are over the moon with what you've achieved. Might even be a bonus in it for you.'

'That would be very welcome. Well, it's goodbye, then.' She held out her hand in the formal fashion.

He raised an eyebrow.

'Hey, Erin!'

He was right. They'd known each other too long for that, and there were no hard feelings now on either side. Nevertheless, it was still a rather awkward two-second embrace.

And it was the worst two seconds of all for the door to swing open and for Brad to walk in.

★　★　★

'For a split second there, I really thought you were going to thump Spencer.'

Brad was driving them back to Norfolk. She was still pinching herself that he was really here. Another shock was to discover that Metal Mickey had made the journey over and — fingers crossed — looked like making it back, too!

'I nearly did.' Brad pulled a face. 'I was eaten up with jealousy.'

'Were you?' she said, delighted. 'But I'd said there was nothing personal left between me and Spencer. Didn't you believe me?'

'Yes, but since that night he dragged you back to Manchester, I was scared stiff that, when you got there, you'd realise what you'd been missing and decide to stay.'

'That's what he thought, as well. And you were both wrong. But Spencer did me a favour by forcing me back, because it made me certain that my old hectic way of life holds no attraction for me anymore. My heart's in Brundenham. I don't ever want to leave again. It's made me absolutely determined to find a way of staying on.'

'Really?'

There was so much released tension in that one word.

'Oh, Brad, I knew it months ago, but never allowed myself to admit it.'

'But you talked about what would happen with the animals when it came to you leaving.'

'Only because I needed to keep my feet on the ground, to keep reminding myself that it was only temporary. I was just preparing myself if it came to the worst. If I had plans in place, the theory was it wouldn't hurt that much when the time came. The trouble was, it hurt like crazy, anyway.'

'A bit like me trying to protect myself from any more disappointments. I didn't want to fall in love with you, Erin.'

Erin stopped breathing for a second.

'I couldn't bear the thought of falling in love with you, and then losing you. But it was too late. I already had. Fallen in love with you, I mean. And I realised that it was up to me not to lose you, that I'd do anything it took to keep you. And it's taken me far too long to admit all that to myself, let alone you.'

'And now you have,' she said softly.

'And now I have. And you can't run away either, because we're doing . . . ' he glanced down at the speedometer ' . . . sixty-eight miles an hour down a motorway!'

'Are you sure?'

He looked again.

'Yep. Sixty-eight. It's heady stuff for Metal Mickey, isn't it!'

'Never thought he was capable. But even if he'd broken down and had come to a standstill, I'd still not be running away, Brad.'

'I wouldn't mind if he did break down right now.' Brad sighed. 'Because I really need to kiss you. Is that an exit sign coming up?'

'No.'

'Where's a traffic jam when you need one? What's happened to all the holiday getaway queues?'

'We've somehow managed to miss them all. Just try to be patient a bit longer.'

Was that really her talking? She was just as impatient as him!

Despite their declaration of love and the promise of kisses ahead, the pendulum was still swinging over her head. How could she secure her longer-term future at Brundenham? She pushed the thought to the back of her mind for now.

But she'd forgotten Brad could read her mind. He reached out and squeezed her hand.

'Something will turn up, just wait and see. I remember that day I found you planting bulbs. You looked so beautiful and at home there. It was breaking my heart to think of those flowers coming up, and you not living there anymore.'

'I kept picturing you living at Owl

Cottage after I'd left. It gave me a sort of comfort, knowing at least you could have the home you wanted, you and Walt.'

'Oh, Erin, I could never have moved in after you'd gone away. That would just have been twisting the knife.'

'While I imagined you seeing the bulbs come up, and hoped you'd think of me! Perhaps even come and find me, wherever I might be . . . '

'I can't tell you what agony it's been while you've been away. I get back after work and open the door to the smell of your perfume. Those post-it reminder notes you use are stuck everywhere, and even the way you arrange stuff in the cupboards is agony. I just had to see you again, to find out if you felt anything for me. I had to see if I could possibly sweep you off your feet and convince you to stay longer than the end of February.'

'Oh, Brad. And I'd only gone away to do the job because the money meant I could stay beyond February. But you would have had no idea of that when you turned up and found Spencer hugging me!'

'That's why, yes, he very nearly did get a thumping. Until I realised what I was seeing was a goodbye hug. A very final goodbye. After that, I could have hugged him!'

'You're not the thumping type anyway,' she said.

She twisted in the passenger seat to gaze at him, ecstatic that he'd done this uncharacteristically impetuous thing of coming to carry her home for Christmas.

'I do get fired up sometimes,' he said, grinning.

'Do I fire you up?' she teased. 'Not in the wanting-to-thump-me way, though!' she hastened to add.

His eyes glittered in the shadowy interior of the moving car.

'What do you think?'

She'd never been really sure until now. Their first few kisses had been sweet and light. Only the kiss at the

October Fayre had given her any real clue, but since then events had conspired to keep them apart.

Now she just wanted to enjoy the luxury of being with him, and the knowledge that they were going home together.

Home! She stretched back in her seat, closed her eyes and gave a deep sigh of contentment.

'Do you want to stop somewhere for some food?' he asked, as they continued bowling along the motorway, managing to avoid the Christmas Eve traffic more by chance than design.

'Mmm. I'm starving. I feel like I've not had a proper meal for weeks and weeks.' Something Brad had cooked especially for her, she meant. 'What's happening at the cottage with the animals?'

'Daph and Pete are popping round to feed the cats and secure the chickens. And Walt's spending the day at theirs. So they're all being well looked-after.'

'That's OK, then. Yes, let's stop and eat,' she agreed.

'And kiss, let me remind you!'

She didn't need reminding!

They came out of the services and headed for the car.

Brad grabbed her hand.

'Last leg. Before I left they were forecasting snow for Norfolk.'

Erin shivered.

'We might even get snowed in.'

'Only if we get there before it starts. Otherwise we'll be snowed out! So let's get a move on, shall we?'

She laughed, feeling so very, very happy.

January Changes

'It's your birthday?' Brad said incredulously on the first day of January.

Erin nodded as she hung up the calendar for the New Year. The snowy scene on the print mirrored the real one outside perfectly. The new calendar looked like being as accurate as the old one.

'Yep, I'm a New Year baby.'

'You're my baby.' He gave her a kiss. 'But I feel awful because I haven't got you a present.'

'Tell me you love me again,' she urged. 'That will do.'

'I love you,' he said, simply and earnestly.

It still made her want to laugh and cry at the same time, hearing those words at long last.

'Can I ask how old?'

'It's a big one. Thirty today.'

'Really? Then you're older than me.

I'm not thirty till later this year.'

'So you're my toy boy!' she teased, but with a grimace. 'I don't like that term very much. When is your birthday, Brad?'

She felt as if they'd known each other for ever, but there was still so much more to learn.

'July fifteenth, Saint Swithin's Day. My mum once told me it rained for forty days and nights after I was born. If she'd known it was going to do that before she registered the birth, she would have named me after him!'

Erin studied him with her head on one side.

'I'm trying to imagine you as a Swithin.' She burst out laughing, causing Walt to run round excitedly. 'It's not working. You're just too . . . too Braddish.'

'You don't mean brattish?'

'No, never brattish. Standoffish, some-times. You can be distant and reserved, and it took far too long for me to know you loved me. But I forgive you every-thing, now that I finally do know.'

'Do you now?' he said, pulling her into his arms. 'That's very magnanimous of you.'

'It's my birthday. I'm feeling magnanimous.'

'And I'm feeling a heel now, because I didn't know. Hey, what about this for an idea . . . ?' He shook his head. 'No, it's not much of a gift.'

'What?'

'A trip to the football.'

'The football?' She hadn't expected that.

'Warned you it wasn't that much of a gift. But I've got a couple of tickets for the Norwich City game this afternoon.'

'Is it still on, with all this weather?'

'Heated pitch.'

'Of course. Well, I'd love to go.'

'Pete and Daph will be delighted to know they've introduced a new fan.'

'Won't they just! But Brad . . . ' She hesitated. 'How will you feel?'

'About going back to watch a professional game?'

She nodded. It was very different

from having a fun kickabout in a five-a-side village tournament. Wouldn't being back in a Premiership stadium bring back too many bad memories?

'I think my cure is total now. And besides, I have been back to a league stadium. Quite recently. You remember suggesting I get involved in the game in some other way?'

She nodded.

'I got in touch with my old club. I even went down to see them just before Christmas. We're in talks about me delivering some kind of occasional training sessions to the youth squad.'

'Oh, Brad, that's fantastic! I'm so pleased; it sounds great for you, and for them.' Another new revelation, she was thinking. 'You never said anything,' she scolded.

'We've got such a lot to catch up, Erin. Come on, let's take Walt out for a long run now if we're going out this afternoon. We'll walk and talk at the same time.'

At the word 'walk', Walt was already

leaping up and down in front of the hook where his lead was hung. The cats threw him supercilious looks, as if to marvel at them doing anything so undignified.

'Apart from the training idea.' Brad resumed the topic of his old club when they were wrapped up and trudging through the snow in the lane, hand in hand. 'They've also suggested I might like to give a few talks on life after football.'

'That's an angle,' Erin said thoughtfully.

'Players retire early. Even without injury or accident curtailing their careers. They're effectively out of a job when they reach forty. But there is life afterwards.'

'As you've proved.' She squeezed his arm.

'Not without you,' he said simply.

She blushed, but knowing the credit was far from hers.

'You'd taken accounts courses before you'd met me. You'd found yourself a new career, and a new job at Greensides.'

'Yes,' he conceded, 'but I wasn't happy, was I? I was still hankering after the past, couldn't see my future at all. I was marking time until I met you. You changed my life around.'

'And you didn't just change mine,' she said. 'You turned it upside-down. Upside-down and head over heels.' She gazed into Brad's eyes. 'I've never been in love before,' she admitted. 'I always imagined that to feel like this it would have to be love at first sight.'

'You mean it wasn't?' Brad stopped, to allow him to take a step back in pretend shock.

'You intrigued me,' Erin admitted. 'I couldn't stop wondering who you were and hoping I'd see you again.'

'I only caught a glimpse of you that first night at the door.'

'And mistook me for your ex-girlfriend!'

'Only for a split second. After that, I was wondering who this beautiful sparky woman was who had snatched my cottage away from under my nose.'

'I hated seeing your disappointment.'

'I went back to my room at Greensides and tried to work out why I wasn't more annoyed. All I could see was your sympathetic face. That rankled me.'

She shook her head.

'No, I soon realised you were uncomfortable with sympathy. When you told me that your ex-girlfriend had been sympathetic immediately after the car accident, and then dropped you, I assumed that was the reason why.'

'Did you? Heavens, no.' He shook his head ruefully. 'I'm a typical man. I love a bit of sympathy in certain circumstances. And if I ever catch a cold, feel free to ladle it on with a big spoon!'

'We'd better start walking again,' she said, stamping her frozen feet in the snow, 'otherwise we'll both end up with flu!'

Brad caught her mittened hand in his and they walked on a bit further.

'As soon as I met you properly, Erin, I wanted you to be attracted to me, not feel sorry for me.'

'I was definitely attracted, but I wondered if I'd ever see you again, and then I did, in the Rosy Leaf.'

'I could hardly believe it was you. You looked so different in your business suit and high heels, your lovely hair pinned up.' He moved to touch it now, streaming over her shoulders from under a bright-red bobble hat.

'And you rushed off before I could talk with you.'

'What an idiot, huh?'

Walt gave a short bark. They broke apart and looked at him.

'What's up, boy?'

Erin answered for him.

'He's telling us to stop slowing down and hugging all the time. We're supposed to be walking!'

'I thought of coming back to Owl Cottage, but I couldn't think of an excuse.' He smiled ruefully, as they headed up the bridle path on one of their favourite circuits round the back of the village. 'I walked up and down

242

your lane several times, you know.'

'Did you? I never saw you.'

'I kept a low profile. It occurred me that you might have thought I was stalking you!'

Erin laughed.

'I'd wondered if you thought that about me! I was drinking tea at Greensides on the day before my meeting with Jim Standing. Suddenly you materialised and walked through the foyer. I could hardly believe my eyes!'

'I never saw you. I couldn't believe mine, when Jim Standing brought you into my office! I was totally bowled over.'

'You didn't show it. You were so controlled and calm. And scarily efficient, with all the figures at your fingertips.'

'It's my job. And you can talk! Stalking in like businesswoman of the year, all cool and professional.'

'It's my job!' she retorted.

But they were grinning at each other.

'Hey, you two!' Erin looked up to see Daph and Pete, and realised, despite all the stopping and starting, they had still managed to walk all the way round the back of the village without realising it.

'We're running off some of our Christmas excesses,' Pete said, jogging half-heartedly on the spot.

'Are we?' Daph queried. 'I thought we were just popping round to see our Karen. Don't suppose they'll even be up yet. It was quite some party last night.'

'And this is my New Year resolution. Keeping fit.' Pete puffed. He stopped, blowing hard, and stood with his hands on his knees. 'Phew, that's enough of that for now. Hello, Walt!' he added, making a fuss of the dog who'd jumped up to lick his face.

'Our New Year resolution is to support Norwich City a bit more,' Erin said. 'Starting with this afternoon.'

'I'd got the tickets before I knew it was Erin's birthday,' Brad said. 'So a trip to the game has ended up serving as her present . . . for now.'

'Is it? Oh, happy birthday, love!'

Daph gave her a hug. 'I won't ask how old, because I'll only be jealous.'

'Yes, many happy returns. And great about the footie!' Pete grinned his crooked-toothed smile at Brad. 'Erin might enjoy it a bit more if you're taking her.'

'I did enjoy it before,' Erin protested. 'It was all a bit new to me.'

She felt Brad's hand curl around hers, and knew he'd remembered that she'd also been upset at the time by their phone conversation. Although afterwards, he'd opened his heart to her. Looking back, it had signalled a change, the real starting point of their journey. So in a very roundabout way, she had a lot to thank Norwich City Football Club for!

'We can all travel together, if you want to,' Daph added, giving Brad and Erin darting looks. 'Unless you'd rather be alone together.'

Brad chuckled.

'You're never alone at a football match! But we'd love to, and perhaps go on for some food afterwards?'

'You're on,' Pete said warmly, thumping his hands together. 'There's that new curry place opened up not far from the ground.'

'If you're having curry, you'd better give the half-time pie a miss.'

'Aw, Daph, we can't. It's traditional!'

'You just spoke about getting fit. Your resolution didn't last long!'

Brad and Erin could hear the conversation continuing after they'd passed.

'They're a pair, aren't they! Will we get to be like them?' he asked.

'Hope so,' Erin said, her heart leaping crazily. Pete and Daph had been together for years and years.

Since Christmas Erin had been living in a bubble. The long-awaited closeness with Brad, their declaration of love, she'd managed to put the real world into hibernation.

She turned her head so as not to let Brad see her change of expression. Because the doubts over their future were waiting to resurface, just as soon as she could face them. There was the problem of how she was going to earn her living if the consultancy work didn't improve. It jeopardised her whole stay in Brundenham — and, she suddenly remembered, she still hadn't contacted the agent over extending the lease on the cottage. She'd have to do that the moment the office reopened after the holidays. If the owner was agreeable, she could afford to commit until June. But after that?

They reached the Rosy Leaf, which had been closed up since Christmas Eve, Brad had already told her. And she could see now for herself the blinds pulled down at the ground floor windows.

'When are Rosie and Oliver due back?'

'Not for about another month,' he said.

'A nice long holiday in the sun will do them good. And they can relax even more knowing you're around upstairs keeping an eye on things.'

With the arrangements made for Erin to take Walt back to Owl Cottage and pick up Brad later from the bedsit on her way round to collect Daph and Pete, they prepared to part.

'Wishing it was you — us — sunning ourselves somewhere warm?' he said.

Erin shook her head firmly.

'All I need is here,' she said, lifting her face for his kiss.

'I knew that,' he said. 'I just wanted to hear you say it!'

February Proposal

Erin was surprised to find that the February page on the calendar included a twenty-ninth day. She hadn't realised or planned that her own leap year would end on a real one! The small print in her Owl Cottage lease document said 'until the last day of February'. So she unexpectedly had one more extra day. It felt like a mini reprieve of sorts.

Should she ring the agent again? She'd rung nearly every day for a month. They kept saying they'd get back to her the second they heard from Owl Cottage's overseas owner.

She'd been annoyed and frantic in turn. OK, so the man was in Hong Kong. but it wasn't Mars, for goodness' sake!

The uncertainty clouded everything. It distracted her from getting to grips with searching for more image consultancy work, although it was difficult to know what more she could do on that front. The website had been given yet another overhaul.

Since tying up any loose ends of jobs started last year, the previous month had only seen a few new enquiries but with no contracts signed as yet. Spencer had forwarded her a glowing thank-you letter from Easyplease Foods, along with an almost apologetic e-mail reminding her that, if she should be thinking of coming back to Manchester in the near future, he would be pleased to offer her more freelance work.

The praise was gratifying, but bitter-sweet. If only the work could have been in Norfolk.

The uncertainty also cast a pall over her future happiness with Brad. Despite his assurances that all would turn out well, Erin preferred things to be signed and sealed.

If Brad was panicking over the bedsit — should Rosie and Oliver sell up — then he was keeping it to himself. But at this rate, the worst-case scenario would be both of them being homeless, although she supposed Brad could always go back to staff digs at the hotel. Back to square one, she thought dismally.

There was also a knock-on effect for Erin to worry about. It meant she couldn't make a decision over her Manchester flat. The person who'd taken on the annual lease from her now wanted to extend it, and she hadn't been able to give them an answer. Erin hated the thought of messing anyone around.

'If you take the plunge, let your flat go, and if you ever find yourself coming back here anyway,' Elaine said, 'you know you'd never be homeless. We'd squeeze you in somehow. And there's always the spare room at Graham's mum's. She loved having you to stay last year.'

'Oh, that's lovely of her to say so, and for your offer. Thanks, sis.'

She knew she was very lucky to have family to fall back on.

'But I know your heart is there, Erin. And I don't think for a moment Brad will be letting you go anywhere any time soon.'

'I hope not,' Erin murmured, as much to herself as to Elaine.

'Chase up that letting agent again,' Elaine ordered. 'Get them to do their job!'

'They've not been very good at it so far, have they? The left hand never did seem to know what the right was doing.'

'No, but when you think about it, that wasn't a bad thing in the beginning. Otherwise Brad would never have turned up that night.'

That was true enough.

Erin made yet another phone call, and was advised by the agent to hang on tight for a few more days. Phone calls, texts, e-mails had all been fired off, and the owner was sure to respond soon.

But the days were dripping away like a leaky tap. And there was not a single place to rent in the village or anywhere near it that was within her limited price range and for so short a term.

Inactivity, she decided, only made things seem worse. She set to and cleaned the cottage from bottom to top. Walt trying to attack the vacuum cleaner always made Erin laugh, while the cats hopped up on to the window-sill and turned their backs until the whole unpleasant affair was over with.

A quick check confirmed that she hadn't missed any calls while the vacuum had been running. Right, now the inside was clean, time to tackle any outside jobs.

Erin wrapped herself up in her puffer coat and the matching yellow and green striped hat and scarf set that Brad had treated her to from the stall outside the Norwich City match.

'A funny sort of birthday gift,' he'd said, 'but the colours really go with your fair hair.'

Even if they'd clashed, Erin would still have been delighted.

'Coming, you three?' she called to

Walt and the cats as she let herself out into the back garden. They didn't need asking twice.

The sky was a brilliant crystal clear blue. It was bitterly cold, but the snow had all gone, and the hens were again venturing into their run to see what insects and other goodies the cold snap had left behind.

Napoleon scratched up something and gave a strange little call. Erin recognised the sound as meaning, 'Come and see this!' and so did his hens.

They dashed over, eagerly winging each other aside in their haste to be first there and secure the treat. Josephine won the day, and triumphantly rolled whatever it was between her beak for a second before swallowing it.

There was a contingency plan for Napoleon and his harem. Pete Carr had always said he'd have them, and the Carrs's married daughter Karen, who lived at the other end of the village, had also offered. She already had the kitten

Tyson, who was now a rather fine-looking, grown-up male cat.

Erin watched Feather and her daughter Mouse prowl over the vegetable garden, bare now but for a few tatty-looking leeks and a couple of faded stalks of brussels sprouts. The cats were very special to her. Poor Feather being dumped on the doorstep in a cardboard box, and pregnant — although she'd had no idea of it at the time. And she had watched Mouse being born, the last and smallest of the litter of three.

Wherever Erin ended up, it had to be somewhere she could take them.

And, then, there was Walt. Another waif and stray with a sorry history.

What would become of him? He had his paws up on the fence now and was sniffing the air across the fields. He loved the countryside and their walks. Brad had said that since coming to live with her, Walt had just been a different dog.

'Yes, Walt, we'll go out properly soon,' she said, going to join him by the fence, resting her hand on his silky head and gazing out across the landscape.

With the days still so short, it was always dark by the time Brad left off work and arrived at the cottage. Fabulous for romantic stargazing, but no good for dog runs in the absolute blackness of the countryside.

So Erin had been walking him by herself during the afternoons. Walking, and turning everything over and over in her mind. And occasionally dreaming of the perfect solution, whatever that might be.

Early on the morning of February 14, Brad rang her as usual before he set off to work. Erin was still sitting at the kitchen window-sill worktop, having breakfast.

'Happy Valentine's Day! Would you allow me to take you to dinner tonight?'

'That sounds very formal!' She laughed. 'But, yes, I'd love it. Any clues to where it might be?'

'Rosie's OK?'

'Of course it is.'

It was her favourite place to eat. Since Rosie and Oliver had returned from holiday, the Rosy Leaf had resumed its usual Monday to Saturday daytime trading hours, and as Rosie's bistro on Friday and Saturday evenings.

Tonight, being a weekday, it wouldn't normally be open, but obviously they must be making an exception because it was Valentine's Day.

With all worries determinedly put on hold for the evening, Erin decided to relish the process of a long, leisurely session of getting ready. Switching on a Miles Davis CD, she listened to the whole album whilst enjoying an extravagantly scented bubble bath.

After several experiments with hairstyles, and pulling faces at herself in the mirror, she brushed it all out, leaving it long, loose and straight. She applied a little bit of makeup, mainly to accentuate her eyes. Familiar with Rosie's dim candlelight, it was easy to disappear into the background shadows.

Following a lengthy examination of

everything in her wardrobe, she finally decided on a simple but elegant, knee-skimming, silky dress in a soft primrose yellow. Perhaps red would have been more in keeping for Valentine's Day, but yellow seemed more appropriate, because it was the optimistic colour of spring and renewed hopes. And also because it reminded her of the primroses that were already budding up in the sheltered border under the window.

She'd noticed them that morning, as well as the tips of the early daffodil leaves that were just starting to poke through the soil. The bulbs that she'd planted last year. The garden, as with all nature, was coming back to life.

Taking a quick last look in the long mirror, Erin declared herself satisfied and headed downstairs.

Napoleon and the girls had already been secured in at dusk. She'd given Walt a good walk round the fields earlier, so he'd be happy to spend the evening relaxing in his basket with his feet up in the air. The cats, too, had curled up on the sofa, one on each cushion like a pair of matching ornaments.

'Right, be good, you lot,' she told them, checking her bag for her keys. 'I'll see you later.'

Her hand was reaching out for the door when the phone started ringing. She whirled round. The number in the display panel was familiar. It was the letting agent. This was a late time to be calling.

With her heart in her mouth, she picked it up.

★　★　★

From the outside, the Rosy Leaf looked warm and inviting. In the window alcove a table for two had been set bistro-style, with a red gingham tablecloth, shining cutlery and gleaming glassware.

In the centre was a china bud vase containing a single red rose, and a chunky white candle decorated down the sides with beads of cold, spilled wax.

It seemed very quiet for Valentine's

Night. When she saw the notice on the door she realised why.

Private party.

'That's us. We're the private party,' Brad explained, who emerged from the kitchen to greet her the moment the bell chimed out.

'Wow!' she breathed.

He looked good enough to eat, she thought, taking in his dark blue suit trousers and lighter blue shirt. He was even wearing a necktie under his white chef's apron, which he was struggling to get off.

'Even better,' she murmured, when he finally had.

He slipped on the matching suit jacket. She hoped he was going to spend lots of time gazing into her eyes across the table, rather than in the kitchen, even though the smells that were wafting through from that direction were mouth-wateringly delicious.

'Wow yourself,' he said as he eased her coat from her shoulders and took in her dress.

The sensation of his eyes roaming over her made her want to melt.

Brad pulled back a chair for her.

'Milady, your supper awaits.'

He dashed back to the kitchen and returned in under a minute with a heated trolley.

'It's all prepared and ready to serve,' he said, 'so we can just sit down and enjoy it. Ta-ra!' he added with a flourish, producing an ice-filled wine bucket.

He lifted the bottle to show her the label.

'Champagne!'

He popped the cork and filled two glass flutes.

'To my one and only love.'

She held her champagne aloft, and they chinked glasses. Brad took a gulp, which was unusual for him. He sat down, cleared his throat, looked at her, and then stood up again.

'What have you forgotten?'

She surveyed the dishes. Everything seemed to be there.

'Nothing.'

The next thing she knew, he was down on his knees at her feet.

'Erin, will you marry me?'

For a crazy, mixed-up minute, Erin couldn't understand why the grandfather clock in the corner continued to beat out steadily, while, for her, time had stood still.

She tried getting to her feet, but her legs didn't want to work either. And there was Brad, his gorgeous, handsome expectant face gazing up at her.

'Marry you?' Her voice came out as a squeak, and then a whisper. 'Oh, Brad, yes, yes, of course I will.'

And then they were up on their feet, until Brad lifted her off hers and swung her round and round. And the kiss that followed made her feel equally giddy.

'Are you sure. Really sure?' he said, when they'd finally calmed down enough to sit down.

'Yes, I'm sure, Brad. I'm not just agreeing to marry you out of sympathy!' she teased, but then turned serious. 'But because I love you very, very much.'

He sat gazing at her, his chin in his hand, and suddenly yelped.

'I forgot the ring! The idea was to present it to you with the sweet course. That's when I planned to propose. But as soon as you got here that all went out of the window, because I knew I couldn't wait that long.'

'Not so measured and reserved all the time, then!'

'Oh, I can do impetuous, Erin . . . as long as I can think it all through beforehand!'

He felt in his jacket pocket and drew out a small jewellery box. He lifted the lid and held it out to her.

She noticed his hand was trembling slightly. She put her own hand around it and peered in the box at a classically cut and set diamond solitaire.

'Oh, Brad, it's absolutely gorgeous!'

'You like it? Really? We can change it if you don't.'

'Don't you dare! I absolutely love it. You chose it, and I'd love it for that reason alone. But it's exactly what I'd have picked myself, you clever, clever man.'

'Let's make sure it fits.' He caught up her hand and gently threaded it on to her finger. 'There.'

'It's perfect.'

'I noticed your sister's engagement ring was a solitaire diamond. And you seem to have similar tastes, so I was hoping I'd get it right.'

Exactly right.

And he'd noticed she wasn't a fan of flashy chunky jewellery. She adored the simplicity of classic pieces.

'I don't know if I can eat anything at the moment,' she said breathlessly, looking at the table. 'I'm too excited.'

'You'd better try.' He glowered lovingly. 'I've been hours slaving away in front of a hot stove! But I know what you mean. I feel the same.'

'Were Rosie and Oliver in on this?' she asked. 'Is that how you talked them into letting you take the place over for the evening?'

'Not the marriage proposal, though they might have guessed about that. But they knew we'd have something important to discuss tonight.'

There was something more, then. She suddenly felt incredibly nervous.

'What?'

Brad had picked up the cutlery for the starter, but placed it back down on the table again.

'Rosie and Oliver definitely want to retire.'

'Oh!' Erin gasped.

He reached for her hand.

'No, it's not bad, Erin, trust me. They've made a suggestion. They want us to run and manage the Rosy Leaf for them.'

'Us?'

'What do you think? Would you like to do it?'

'Like it? I'd love it!'

Married and not only living together but working together, too. Her mind whirled with the exciting possibilities plus any potential pitfalls.

'Do we know enough to run a café full time? What about your job at the hotel?'

'We'd need to sort all those details out. I thought I'd carry on at Greensides Monday to Friday, at least to begin with. Rosie and Oliver would see us through the practicalities. We've already picked up a lot since doing the Sundays.'

'Was that behind the idea of asking us to do them to begin with?'

'Possibly. Or perhaps it occurred to them once they saw how much we enjoyed it and how successful it was. But you do see what it means, Erin?'

'Yes,' she breathed inaudibly, unable to speak for the rush of emotions coursing through her. They had a future there!

'I'd like to continue opening up Rosie's as a bistro on weekend evenings.'

'With your food, it'd be a crime not to.'

She'd finally started eating, and now she felt ravenous.

'It's the relief,' Brad told her, who

was also tucking in.

'It's your cooking!' She smiled. 'I can't believe this is all happening, can you?' With new ideas already spinning round her head, she couldn't give him time to answer. 'We could start Sunday openings this year right from Easter. That's when the tourist season begins. We'd possibly need some help though? Would Claire . . . ?'

'She's already said she'd be happy to do as many hours as she can fit in around her hotel shifts.'

'And Daph's daughter Karen is looking for part-time work to fit in round the school hours. She might be interested in some weekday shifts.' A sideways thought crept in. 'Brad, did you know all along that Rosie and Oliver had this idea in mind?'

'Sort of,' he admitted. 'Nothing definite, but Rosie had dropped a few hints into our conversations. I knew their holiday away was to give them some thinking time about the café's future. But I didn't want to tell you,

Erin, in case it came to nothing, or they just decided to sell up. It would have been heartbreaking to know what might have been. Do you forgive me keeping it a secret?'

'I'll think about it!' she teased. 'On the way home.'

'I'm glad you didn't drive down here,' Brad said once he'd checked round, locked up, and they were standing outside the café. The evening was dry, sharp and clear. 'I'd much rather walk you back. Sure you won't be too cold?' he said, lifting the collar of her coat, and then pressing his palms to her cheeks and drawing her close for a kiss.

'Not now,' she murmured.

Linking arms, they made their way along the silent street. The full moon was so light, the torch Erin kept in her bag was unnecessary.

'We're never going to forget this Valentine's night, are we?' she whispered. 'Do you feel any different? Inside, I mean. I do.'

'And so you should. Not only are you going to be a co-manager of Brundenham's most successful café, let me remind you that you're also an engaged woman now!'

'As if I could forget,' she said, holding up her hand so the ring caught the moonlight.

'You're very nearly Mrs Cavill. Just as soon as we can arrange the wedding.'

She stopped to glance back at All Saints' church tower. How perfect would it be to get married there.

'Erin Cavill. Brad and Erin Cavill. Mr and Mrs Cavill,' she practiced. It tasted good on her tongue. 'And I feel different knowing this is our home now. Our village. The place where we'll work and live.'

'Talking of where we'll live,' Brad said, 'we'll manage up in the bedsit after we're married, won't we? I know it'll be a squeeze, but once we put together my salary and the café earnings, I'm sure we can find some place else local to rent.'

'It must be somewhere in Brundenham, mustn't it? Don't you feel as if we've already put our roots down in this Norfolk soil.'

'I do,' he said, gathering her close.

They'd arrived back at Owl Cottage, and Erin pressed her fingers to Brad's chilled lips.

'Listen! Did you just hear an owl?'

'Yes,' he whispered back, then held up a hand. 'Ah, there it goes again.'

'I heard one on my first night here. There!' She stopped as an answering call came from a different direction.

'That is definitely what you'd call the sound of romance in the air,' Brad said when the duet had ended.

'Let's not go inside for a minute more,' she whispered, pausing on the step with the key already in her hand. 'I just want to stand and remember.'

It was the exact same spot where she'd stood almost a year ago, facing the door with the key in her hand, on the brink of her new life. She relived her feelings of anticipation and excitement, tinged with nervousness and trepidation. It had been more of a leap into the unknown than she could have ever imagined.

Not everything had gone entirely to plan, but then if they had, her life would not have ended up this rich. The last twelve months had turned out to be the happiest, the most important, the most memorable twelve months of her life.

Brad stood behind her, his arms curled around her shoulders, so her head rested against his chest.

'Happy?' he murmured into her hair.

'Happy!' she confirmed. 'And, guess what? The agent rang just as I was coming out this evening. He's heard from the owner at last, and he's willing to extend the lease on Owl Cottage for another year at least!'

Brad spun her round, his smile as broad as hers.

'You! You sat on that news all evening!'

'See? You're not the only one who can keep a secret!' she told him smugly. 'Fancy living here after we're married? It'll still be quite a squeeze . . . ' She broke off, laughing breathlessly as Brad held her tight and spun her round.

If the last twelve months had turned out to be beyond her wildest dreams, then next year looked set to get even better.

THE END

We do hope that you have enjoyed reading this large print book.

Did you know that all of our titles are available for purchase?

We publish a wide range of high quality large print books including:
Romances, Mysteries, Classics
General Fiction
Non Fiction and Westerns

Special interest titles available in large print are:
The Little Oxford Dictionary
Music Book, Song Book
Hymn Book, Service Book

Also available from us courtesy of Oxford University Press:
Young Readers' Dictionary
(large print edition)
Young Readers' Thesaurus
(large print edition)

For further information or a free brochure, please contact us at:
Ulverscroft Large Print Books Ltd.,
The Green, Bradgate Road, Anstey,
Leicester, LE7 7FU, England.
Tel: (00 44) 0116 236 4325
Fax: (00 44) 0116 234 0205

Other titles in the
Linford Romance Library:

HUSHED WORDS

Angela Britnell

Cassie, a struggling single mother, and Jay, a wealthy financier, share a holiday romance in Italy; when fate throws them together again their sizzling passion rekindles. Cassie's family problems combined with Jay's fear of commitment and growing dissatisfaction with his lifestyle make their idea of a future together a dream. Jay can't ask for a second chance with Cassie until he discovers a new direction in life and lays it all on the line with the woman he loves.